About the Author

Jennifer McCoy Blaske has been writing since she was in fifth grade, when her mother would come into her room asking her to please stop typing because she was keeping everybody awake.

She has had over fifteen short stories and articles published in six different magazines. In addition, she had an essay included in the book anthology *Humor for a Teacher's Heart.* This is her first book, but not her last.

Jennifer has been playing the piano for weddings and other events in the Atlanta area since 2009. She is married and has three kids, yet she continues to insist that this book is fiction.

ISBN-13: 978-1535554619
ISBN-10: 1535554614

www.PianoJenny.com

October 20, 2016

Diane,
    I hope you enjoy
the book – I bet you
will relate to some of
it! :)
                God bless,
        Jennifer McCoy Blaske

CONFESSIONS
OF A WEDDING
MUSICIAN MOM

Jennifer McCoy Blaske

Dedicated in loving memory to my mother,
Virginia Judith McCoy.

One

Summer vacation was almost over and I still hadn't gotten completely used to grocery shopping with two kids under the age of eight. For one thing, everything seemed to take about three times longer than it did when I went shopping by myself. For another …

"Angela!" I took a can of sliced peaches off the shelf and put it in the shopping cart. "Stop squeezing the marshmallows!"

"But it feels so good to squeeze something so big and squishy." Her fingers lingered on the bag. She gave it one final squish before pulling away her hand.

"Why is there a water squirter in our cart?" I picked up a green water pistol that was wedged between a gallon of milk and a box of Cheerios.

"That was Danny!" Angela shot her index finger toward her little brother's face. "He tried to sneak that in when you weren't looking!"

"I did not!"

"Yes you did! I saw you!"

"Where did you get this?" I looked up and down the aisle. "I don't see any toys here."

"Oh, it wasn't here," said Angela. "I think it was about two aisles back … or three. Or maybe four."

I stared at the water pistol and sighed. I was debating whether or not I wanted to drag everybody back through the store in the hopes of finding the water pistol shelf.

"So are we gonna keep it? Are we?" Danny asked.

"No. No, we are not going to keep it." I glanced around to make sure no one was looking as I tucked the water pistol between two cans of jellied cranberry sauce … hoping it didn't make me a terrible person.

"Come on." I pushed the cart around the corner toward the produce section. "We're almost done."

"Ooh, Mom," Danny cooed as we approached a display of small white tubes with apple smiley faces on them. "Can I have these? Everyone in school has them. Can I have one? Please?"

"What is it?" I picked up a tube and frowned at the smiley faces. "Toothpaste?"

"No," said Angela. "They're Fruit Smooshers."

"Fruit … Smooshers?"

"It's smooshed-up fruit, and you squeeze it right into your mouth," Angela explained.

"So can I get it?" asked Danny.

I looked at the price of these little tubes which undoubtedly contained little, if any, actual fruit, and winced. "No, I don't think …"

"Look at these!" Danny picked up a bag of chocolate-covered raisins and waved it at me. "I want to get these instead."

"She said no." Angela tried to tug the bag out of his hand. "Put it down."

"Leggo!" Danny yanked the bag. "She said no about the Fruit Smooshers not these. Mom!"

Angela lunged forward and started wrestling Danny for the bag. "She meant that she didn't want you to …"

"SHUSH!!" I ordered as I pried their fingers away and slammed the bag on the shelf. "We are not getting anything that's not on my list. I don't want either of you to …"

"Heather?"

I turned around, startled. I was half-expecting to see a store employee ready to escort my family off the premises while firmly informing us to please meet our grocery needs elsewhere in the future.

Instead, I saw a dark-haired woman about my age. She was peering at me curiously. The baby in her shopping cart was wearing a pink headband, sitting in a floral cart cover.

The baby looked so blissfully still—and quiet. I was envious.

"Aren't you Heather Collins?" The woman was studying me. "Did you go to Johnston College?"

"Huh? Uh … yeah. I am, and I did. My married name, my name now, is Heather Hershey." Did I know this person? She didn't look familiar.

"I knew it!" she said. "I'm Catherine Stephens! We were on the same hall freshman year. I was Laurie Sutcliffe's roommate."

"Oh … oh, right." I was starting to remember. Laurie Sutcliffe was known in the dorm for being able to tie a cherry stem into a knot with her tongue. Catherine, on the other hand, had no such talents that I was aware of.

"I transferred to Hunter City College after freshman year, so I wasn't at Johnston very long," said Catherine.

"But I remember you. You look exactly the same as you did back then."

"Thank you." I frowned. Maybe that wasn't a compliment.

"This is Lexi." Catherine gestured toward her baby. "She just turned seven months and she …" Her voice trailed off as she gazed past me. "Are those your children playing catch with the apples?"

I whipped around. "Angela! Danny! Put those down and get over here!"

"It was Danny's idea," Angela declared as she set the apple down and walked toward me.

"Was not!"

"How old are they?" Catherine asked.

She was probably wondering how much longer she had until her sweet, quiet—and easy to immobilize—Lexi turned into one of these out of control creatures.

"Angela's eight and Danny just turned six." I glanced over my shoulder at them. "Angela, what are you doing with those bananas?"

Angela looked at me. "Weighing them," she said, as if she was surprised that I had to ask.

"Aw, cool!" Danny's eyes grew big. "I wanna weigh something too! What can I weigh?"

"Wait your turn." Angela plopped a second bunch of bananas on the scale.

"Hey, I know! Let's weigh a watermelon!" Danny took off running down the aisle.

"NO!" I told them. "No weighing produce!"

They both looked at me, shocked.

"Why not?" Danny asked.

"Just … just put the bananas back," I said. "No, actually, put them in the cart. I need to get bananas anyway. No, not both bunches. Just one."

"You were the piano player, I remember," Catherine said.

"Huh?" I dreaded the havoc that could ensue if I took my eyes off the kids, but I turned back to her anyway. "Oh, oh yes, I guess I was." It was funny to be called that. I'd almost forgotten about it. It was strange that something which used to be such a big part of my life now seemed like a distant memory.

"I always thought that was neat," said Catherine. "Being a music major seemed like it was so much more interesting than being, I don't know, a business major or something."

"Oh yeah," I said. "It was, uh … pretty interesting." It was interesting while it lasted anyway. I didn't tell her that I ended up getting my degree in business.

"I have to go to the bathroom," Danny announced.

I turned around. "What? Didn't I tell you to go before we left?"

"I did." He shifted his weight from one foot to the other. "Now I gotta go again."

I looked helplessly toward the bathrooms on the other side of the store. "Can't you just wait a few minutes till we get home? We're almost finished."

He swished his head back and forth. "I really gotta go."

I bleakly turned to Catherine. "Well, it sounds like we need to go. Thanks for saying hi. Your baby is beautiful."

"Thank you. It was good to see you." Catherine pushed little Lexi off toward the dairy section.

"Come on." I wearily turned the cart around and started trudging across the store.

Angela was rummaging through a clearance bin of pool toys as I stood outside the men's restroom waiting for Danny. I kept hearing Catherine's voice in my head: *You were the piano player.*

"Ooh, can we get this Mommy?" Angela waved a red and white swim torpedo at me.

"No."

You were the piano player.

"I'm done." Danny strutted out of the bathroom with a two-foot piece of toilet paper stuck to his shoe.

"Umm …" I said. "You might want to check your shoe, Danny."

"Huh? Oh." He lifted up his foot, peeled off the toilet paper, and threw it on the floor.

"No!" I said. "Go back to the bathroom and throw it in the trash. And wash your hands again."

"What about this Mommy?" Angela was waving a swim noodle around. Then she whacked me on the head with it. "Oh, sorry."

"Ow!" I said. "Angela, put it back. We're not buying any pool toys today."

"I'm done." Danny emerged from the bathroom a second time. His zipper was down and his fly was pooching out, displaying a hint of red Spiderman underwear.

"Oh, for heaven's sake." I leaned forward and zipped Danny back up. "Okay, I think we're actually done. Let's go check out."

You were the piano player.

"Hey Mommy, can we get candy?" Danny asked.

"No," I said over my shoulder as I loaded two jugs of milk onto the conveyor belt. "No candy."

"Are plastic bags okay?" asked the cashier.

"What about gum?" Angela snatched a pack of Bubble Yum off the shelf.

"No!" I yelled.

The cashier looked shocked. "You don't want plastic bags? Well, then, is paper okay?"

"No!" I said. "I mean yes, plastic is fine. Whatever." I grabbed the gum from Angela and put it on the shelf. "Angela, we're not buying any more …" I stopped in my tracks. There was a *Vintage Bride* magazine next to the gum. *Four Mistakes to Avoid When Choosing Your Ceremony Music* was splashed across a photo of a piano keyboard with a red rose lying on it.

"So … then, which one. Paper or plastic?" The cashier sounded annoyed.

"Uh … plastic. Plastic's fine." I plucked the magazine off the rack. I studied it for a moment before slowly placing it back where it belonged.

You were the piano player.

Yes, I thought to myself. Yes I was.

* * *

When we got home I hauled in all the groceries. Then I microwaved three hot dogs and a bowl of baked beans for our lunch.

After we finished eating the kids ran off and I headed down to the basement. I scanned the shelves full of boxes until I found the one labeled *Heather's Piano Music*.

I lugged it upstairs and landed it next to the piano with a thud. Staring at the box warily, I wondered if I should dare open the lid and unleash my former life.

My parents bought the piano for me when I was eleven. I'd heard Bryon Griffin play "The Entertainer" at a school talent show and I was so entranced that I begged my parents for a piano and lessons. It took months, but they finally realized that I wasn't going to back down.

These days, the piano was basically a piece of decorative furniture in my living room. We'd kept it tuned, although I'd barely played it in years. The one exception was that I'd learned to play the theme song to *Millie Mallard's Pond of Fun* to amuse the kids when they were younger. It was their favorite TV show.

I took a deep breath. In one movement I whipped the lid off the box and whirled it aside as I tipped the contents onto the carpet.

After a few seconds of reverence, I gingerly touched the pile of books. They represented my old life—the life that I'd told myself for years that I didn't really want anyway.

I gently fanned some of the books across the carpet. It was like going through photo albums with pictures of people you hadn't seen or spoken to in ten years. It was so long ago, and things were so different back then. It felt like another lifetime.

I studied the books I'd dumped on the floor. I eventually opened my Bach inventions. The pages were stuffed with sixteenth notes, trills, and tricky fingerings. I set that aside and thumbed through a book of Debussy preludes which looked just as scary, if not worse.

It was hard to believe that I used to be able to play this music. What was I thinking? Could I really pick up the piano again after all these years—and then actually find people who would hire me to play for them?

The excitement I'd felt after we left the grocery store was fading fast. I put the Bach and Debussy books back in the box and started half-heartedly leafing through some of the other books.

As I opened my yellow Schemer edition of Chopin's preludes, I noticed some cursive writing in black ink on the inside cover. It was dated the month I graduated from high school.

Congratulation, Heather!

I am so proud of you and all that you have accomplished over the years. It has been such a wonderful pleasure to teach you and I wish you the best. I know you will go far wherever your love for music takes you.

Mrs. Lillian Casey

I'd totally forgotten that Mrs. Casey gave me the Chopin preludes as a graduation gift because I'd played the "Raindrop Prelude" for a recital and liked it so much. I gently flipped through the pages before turning back to the inside cover to read the inscription one more time.

Wow. How could I let Mrs. Casey down?

* * *

On Saturday morning the kids got their bowls of cereal and took them to the couch in the family room to watch TV. I made a bagel and poured a glass of orange juice before sitting down at the kitchen table with my husband, Steve.

"I've decided to become a wedding pianist," I announced. I hadn't wanted to tell him anything until I'd had a few days to ponder the idea and devise a plan. Now it all came bursting out.

Steve set down his coffee cup. "You're what?"

"I've decided to become a wedding pianist. I've ordered business cards and everything! They look really great. There's a picture of a baby grand piano and my name and number in red ink. I've got two hundred of them coming in the mail next week."

"Two hundred?" Steve looked slightly dazed. Or maybe he was wondering if he was dreaming. "Heather, I don't understand. When was the last time you even *played* the piano?"

"That's the point." I was getting excited. "This can give me a real reason to start playing again ... and make money doing it."

Steve looked at me and blinked a couple times. I think he was still half-asleep.

"And wait till you see this!" I got the laptop from the living room, put it on the kitchen table, and started typing. I navigated to the listing I'd placed on a site called Wedding Wild and turned the laptop toward Steve. "What do you think of that?"

He squinted at the screen. "Isn't that your Glamour Shots photo from ten years ago?"

Had it really been that long? "Well ... sure, but it's a great photo, isn't it? And anyway, I look the same now. In fact, that's exactly what the woman I knew from college who I saw at the store the other day told me … that I look the same as I did then!"

"You don't look like this, though." Steve frowned at the screen. "I don't think you ever looked like that. You have gobs of makeup on in this photo, and your hair is … uh … kind of poofy."

"Well, forget about the photo." I waved my hand. "I can always change that later. Read the rest of it!"

Steve looked at the screen and began reading out loud. "Live music makes a wedding elegant and memorable. Heather Hershey's piano music will make your special day magical as she plays from her vast repertoire …" He stopped and looked at me. "Vast repertoire?" His eyes narrowed. "Do you have *any* repertoire right now? I mean, you're not planning on playing the theme song from *Millie Mallard's Pond of Fun* as the bride walks down the aisle, are you?"

I crossed my arms. "I'm perfectly capable of playing a lot more than that you know. And I plan to learn plenty of new songs. In fact, I just ordered a book of wedding music yesterday." I leaned across the table toward him. "Oh, I want so badly for this to work. What do you think? Please tell me I'm not crazy."

Steve sipped his coffee and looked at me for a moment. He looked at the screen and blinked a few times. "Well, this is … really something. And your timing is uncanny."

"My timing? What do you mean?"

Steve heaved a long sigh. "Yeah, I was trying to figure out when to tell you. I wasn't sure if it was worse to tell you when you were in a bad mood, or wait until you were in a good mood and risk ruining it."

My face fell. "Tell me what?"

"They called a meeting at the office yesterday afternoon. Our health insurance premiums are going up next month."

I frowned. "How much?"

He paused. "Two hundred forty-three dollars."

"Two hundred forty-three dollars a month!" I yelped. "Why?"

"Apparently the insurance company just jacked the price up. They tried shopping around, but all the insurance companies are raising their rates, so they say." He shrugged.

"Two hundred forty-three dollars," I murmured as I glanced at the laptop. I was thinking about the costs of the premium listing on Wedding Wild and the extra-thick laminated business cards. Never mind that I'd already started looking into getting a website which would be another substantial cost.

Money had been tight for us since Angela was born. Steve had a decent job that he really enjoyed, but technical writers don't bring in that much money. And, of course, stay-at-home moms bring in no money at all.

We'd always managed, and we were certainly never in any danger of losing our house or having the water shut off. But there wasn't any room for unexpected expenses, and there was nothing we could really cut back on.

Well, okay, we probably spent more on food than we should have. During Steve's bachelor days he survived on ham, mushroom, and Swiss omelets, along with strawberry Pop-Tarts and a lot of fast food. Aside from occasionally making one of his omelets, he had no interest in cooking. And I hated to cook. Or rather, I didn't know how to cook. So we went out to eat and ordered takeouts fairly often.

Anyway, the point was that this two-hundred-plus increase starting—what did Steve say, next month?—was going to be a pretty big deal.

It took me a moment to get over the shock. "Well," I said slowly, "then, this is perfect. Once the wedding jobs start coming in, I'll be making us extra money."

"Yeah." Steve paused for a minute. "And if it doesn't end up working out, we can always talk about you going back to your old job."

I choked on a sip of orange juice. When I was finally finished coughing, I said, "I'm sorry, what did you say?"

"Well, you know, it doesn't have to be the same exact job. But you could go back to doing something like that again."

I used to work in the payroll/accounts receivable department of a consulting firm. I got the job because a friend of my father happened to be hiring the month after I graduated from college. I stayed because the pay was decent and I got along with my co-workers. But probably the biggest reason I stayed was that I didn't have any idea about what I could do instead. As the years went by, I became increasingly restless. I was all too happy to quit to become a stay-at-home-mom after Angela was born.

I glanced down at the half-eaten bagel on my plate and realized that I'd lost my appetite. How did this conversation go from me being thrilled about actually playing the piano again to facing the horrible possibility of being bored out of my mind reporting invoices in a stuffy office again?

"But …" I sputtered, my eyes darting anxiously toward the website on the laptop.

"Oh, don't worry." Steve gestured toward the screen. "I'm just saying that can be our plan B if this wedding thing doesn't happen to work out." He took another sip of coffee, looking confident that any potential problems had just been solved.

That settled it for me. There was no way I was going back to an office job. My brand new career as a wedding pianist would have to work.

Two

It was about an hour before Steve was due home and I was trying to figure out what to make for dinner. I stared at the open pantry, rapped my fingers against the door for a few seconds, and then decided to check the refrigerator again.

When I opened the refrigerator I realized that, unfortunately, nothing new had materialized since I'd looked inside it two minutes ago. I shut the door and went back to staring into the pantry.

I debated whether or not to call Steve and ask him to pick up something on the way home. But I'd already done that two days ago, and you can only get away with that so many times.

I knew I should learn how to cook one of these days. But thinking about it made it seem so daunting.

I never cooked while I was growing up, never. My mother was a fantastic cook, and something of a perfectionist. She never let me and my brother anywhere near her while she was cooking.

I grew up thinking that cooking was something really, really difficult that I would completely mess up if I ever dared try it. I was never quite able to recover from that feeling, not that I ever tried very hard.

"I have a magic trick to perform," Angela announced.

"A magic trick?" I asked as I pushed aside a package of paper towels in the hopes of finding something hidden. I turned away from the pantry which was beginning to annoy me with its unwillingness to produce something new.

Angela was confidently staring up at me through her glasses. "This is called the disappearing marble." She was holding a marble up in one hand and a paper cup in the other. "See … I drop the marble into the cup … abracadabra!" Very slowly, with her left fingers tightly clenched and her face scrunched in concentration, she turned the cup over. Nothing fell out.

"Very nice," I said, applauding.

"Wait, there's more." She waved her right hand in the air. Then she reached behind my ear and pulled out a blue marble.

I laughed. "I love it. Did you show that to your brother?"

Her eyes lit up. "Hey Danny!" She ran out of the room. "Danny I have something to show you! I have something to show you!"

I turned back to the pantry and reached behind a box of crackers. As if by some miracle, I saw a box of pancake mix. I grabbed it just as the phone rang. I snatched the phone from the kitchen counter and walked back to the pantry. "Hello."

"Hi," a female voice said. "Is this Heather Hershey?"

"Yes it is." Oh good, there was still plenty of mix left. I set it down on the counter and started hunting behind the instant oatmeal and a box of tea bags in search of pancake syrup. Aha, here was a fresh bottle. I wedged the phone between my ear and shoulder as I began peeling the plastic off the top.

"My name is Emily," said the voice, "and I'm looking for someone to play the piano for our wedding on October twentieth."

The bottle of syrup tumbled out of my hand and landed right on my foot. Ouch ouch ouch ouch.

"Oh!" I said, trying to sound delighted as I doubled over and grimaced in pain. "Yes. I'd love to play for your wedding." What do I say next? I thought, still wincing at the pain in my toe.

It had only been two weeks since I put up my listing on Wedding Wild, and I hadn't been expecting anyone to actually call me this quickly. I had this vague notion of people eventually seeing my web listing or business card and wanting to hire me, but I actually had no idea *how* I was going to get them to that point. Do I beg her to hire me? Talk about my vast repertoire and hope that she doesn't ask exactly *how* vast my repertoire is? Clearly, I hadn't thought the process through.

"Uh …" Emily hesitated, obviously figuring that she would have to steer this phone call herself. "It's going to be held at the Twin Lakes Country Club in Bridgeville."

Of course! The location! Why didn't I think of that? I rushed over to the magnetic note pad on the refrigerator and scribbled down "Twin Lakes CC October something."

"We're having the ceremony upstairs," said Emily, "and then afterward the cocktail hour will be in the Grand …"

"I do *not* have another marble Danny!" Angela shrieked. "There is just *one* marble!"

Oh no. The kids were in the family room next to the kitchen and there was no door between us to close.

" … which also has a piano in it." Emily went on. "We were thinking of having …"

Do I tell this woman to hold on for a moment while I go kill my children? No, no. I didn't dare let go of my first lead, not even for a few minutes. I dashed out of the kitchen, through the family room, and down the hallway, hoping the kids wouldn't see me.

"I already told you!" Angela yelled. "There is *not* another marble!"

I ran faster down the hallway as Angela's screams were getting louder. "Hey, don't touch that! Get away from me! You're ruining everything Danny!"

"We were hoping for some upbeat songs, you know, things that are a little more modern," said Emily, oblivious to the obstacle course I was running. "We don't want the same old tired songs that you always hear at weddings."

I darted into my bedroom, shut the door, and locked it.

"OWW!! Mom, Angela hit meee!!"

The sound of little running feet was getting nearer. I desperately looked around my bedroom. There was no escape unless I wanted to climb out a window. I unlocked the door and scurried back down the hallway, making shooing motions at Danny. I opened the front door and ran along our front path into the driveway.

"I'm sorry, is this a bad time?" Emily asked. "Maybe you should call me back when …"

"No!" I frantically blurted out. "Nope, not a bad time at all. That's just the, uh … TV in the next room." I took a deep breath. "So then, um …" Oh crap. I had no idea what we'd been talking about. I pressed my fingers against my forehead. "I'm sorry. What were we saying?"

"I was telling you that we wanted some upbeat, modern songs," Emily said dryly.

This was not good. I was losing her.

"Yes, of course," I said quickly. "There are plenty of those we could choose from, like, well …" What modern songs would be good for a wedding? Everything I could think of off the top of my head was classical. "Why don't you think about it, and then let me know which songs you want."

"Okay," said Emily, a touch of doubt in her voice. "So then, what would your price be?"

Price? I had no idea what my prices were. I kept putting off deciding because I didn't have any idea what the going rate was, and I'd thought I would have more time to think about it.

With a jolt of panic, I realized that I wasn't even exactly sure what she wanted to hire me for. Didn't she say something about a cocktail hour? Did she want me to play for the cocktail hour and the ceremony, or just one or the other? Between sprinting wildly around the house and trying to block out all the screaming, I wasn't sure what was going on.

"Mom!" Danny yowled, running out the front door. The screen door slammed behind him as he came barreling toward me. "Angela hit me! And then when I told her not to hit me she *shoved* me!"

"Um, my price is … um," I stammered, "… my price …"

"MOM!" Danny ran up the driveway, arms flailing. "Don't you hear me? Angela hit me! And *shoved* me! Hit me and shoved me! Hit me and shoved me! Hit me and

…" He tripped, fell forward, and lay on his stomach sobbing in the grass. "Mah-hah-haaaahm! I fell! I think I'm bleeding!"

"How long have you been playing for weddings?" Emily sounded suspicious.

"Well …" I said, eying Danny, "well, see, I, um … I haven't exactly played for any *actual* weddings … yet … but I …"

"Thank you," Emily said abruptly. "I'll keep looking. Have a nice day."

"No! No, wait!" I yelled into the phone. "Being new at this means I have to try harder! Wait!" I heard the click of her hanging up, but I kept talking anyway. "Give me a chance! Don't go, don't go, don't … oh, forget it." I hung up the phone and heaved a sigh. It was too late, obviously.

"I'm bleeding!" Danny was still sobbing, lying on his stomach and kicking his feet on the ground. "I'm bleeding! This is Angela's fault!"

I walked over and sat down on the grass next to him. I gently scooped him up and placed him in my lap. "I don't see any blood." I kissed the top of his head and brushed the debris off his legs. "Just dirt. I think you're going to be fine."

Danny looked up at me and sniffed.

"Come on, guy," I said, helping him to his feet. "Let's go inside and make some pancakes for dinner, okay?"

"Okay," he sniffled. "Can I go get Bunny-Bun first?"

"Of course."

As I helped Danny hobble back to the house, I thought, well, so far, my new career isn't exactly getting off to a great start.

Three

"Hey, kids." I knocked on the playroom door a couple times before entering. "I need to talk to you guys for a minute."

"Are we in trouble?" Danny asked.

"Oh no, you're not in trouble." I gathered up a few toys from the couch and set them down on the floor so I could sit down. My eyes narrowed. "Wait a minute. Should you be?"

"Uh-uh," said Danny, vigorously shaking his head.

"Okay then." I held my arms out. He climbed in my lap and Angela sat down next to me. "I've got some exciting news. I'm starting a brand new job."

"A job?" Angela seemed incredulous. "You?"

"That's right," I said.

"Doing what?" Angela asked.

"Babysitting?" Danny piped up.

"Nope," I said.

"Oh, I know," said Angela, as if she'd solved a great mystery. "You're going to be one of those ladies who goes to people's houses and cleans them!"

"What? No!"

"Really? Huh." Angela tapped her finger against her lips, thought for a moment, and then shrugged. "Well, then what *are* you going to do?"

"Yeah, what?" Danny looked equally puzzled.

"Sheesh!" I said. "I am quite capable of doing things other than taking care of kids and cleaning up, you know."

They stared at me blankly.

"So what *are* you going to do?" Angela asked again.

I'd been hoping for a better buildup, but I still managed to find my enthusiasm. "I'm going to play the piano for weddings!"

They continued to stare at me.

"So you're going to start taking piano lessons?" Danny was confused.

"Aren't you a little old to learn how to play a musical instrument?" asked Angela.

"No …" I said, my smile fading. "I mean, I *took* piano lessons for years. I *know* how to play the piano. I went to college on a music scholarship." I peered at them. "Didn't you guys know about any of this?"

"Wow!" Angela breathed, her eyes getting big. "You went to *college* Mommy?"

"No." Danny nudged her. "I think she's just kidding."

"Oh." Angela turned to me and started laughing. "Ha, ha! Good one!"

"Hee hee hee," said Danny with a little snort through his nose.

"Wait a minute." I looked back and forth at them. "That's not a joke. I really *did* go to college. I *graduated* from college!"

"Really?" Angela's laughter suddenly disappeared.

"Wow." Danny gazed at me.

"So what happened?" Angela asked.

"Happened?" I said. "What do you mean?"

"Why couldn't you find a job?" she asked. "Or did you just decide that you never wanted to work?"

"I *did* work!" I was indignant. "I mean, I still *do* work. I just don't ... oh for heaven's sake!"

This conversation was taking a very strange turn. I took a deep breath and tried again. "Okay, the point is that I've decided to become a wedding pianist. I'll be playing the piano at wedding ceremonies. Isn't that neat?"

"Yeah," said Angela. "I didn't even know that the song from *Millie Mallard's Pond of Fun* was a wedding song."

I sighed. "It's not. I'll be playing different songs at the weddings."

"That sounds really fun," said Angela. "Can we come with you?"

"Nope," I told her. "But here's what you can do, and this is what I wanted to talk to you about. People are going to start calling me about playing for their weddings, so it's really important that I'm not disturbed with any noises or distractions during those phone calls. So, how about we have some sort of signal to make it clear that I'm on the phone about a wedding job?"

You would think that *holding* the phone up to my head and speaking into it should be enough indication that I needed to be left alone. However, eight years of parenting experience had led me to believe that this was not necessarily the case.

The kids pondered for a moment.

"How about this?" Danny bent his arms at the elbows and flapped them like he was doing the chicken dance.

"Hmm." Somehow, I couldn't picture myself giving a price quote for a wedding at the Ritz-Carlton while running into the next room flapping my arms.

"No, that's silly!" said Angela, putting her hands on her hips. "It has to be something more like …" She thought for a moment, then stood up and starting doing jumping jacks. "How about this? Would this be easy for us to notice?"

"Uh," I said, raising my eyebrows. I wasn't sure if panting and gasping for breath while taking a call was quite the way to go, either.

"How about this?" Danny squatted on the floor and jumped up repeatedly, like a frog.

"You know, I'm not even sure that I could do that," I said.

"That's too low to the ground. We won't see her! How about this?" Angela reached behind her back, grabbed her right heel, and started jumping up and down on her left foot.

"Oh yeah! But add this!" Danny started doing the same thing while patting his head with his left hand.

"Like this?" Angela copied him.

"Yeah! But lift your arm higher!"

"Like this? Ow!"

"You know," I said, watching them both stumbling around smacking their own heads, "I appreciate the ideas, but somehow this is not quite what I had in mind."

Angela stopped. "Why don't you just make a sign?"

Now that wasn't a bad idea. "Yeah, maybe that could work."

"I can do it!" Angela ran over to the craft shelf, unaware of the two books she'd stepped on while getting there.

She came back with a piece of red card stock and some markers.

Meanwhile, Danny was still hopping around and whacking himself on the head.

"Danny, you can stop hopping now," said Angela. "I'm gonna just make a sign."

"Okay." Danny stopped. He looked relieved.

Angela wrote for a minute. She held up the sign and said, "Ta-da!" The crooked red lettering on her sign read:

**Moms on the phone —
evrybuddy SHUT UP!!**

"Angela!" I said. "Could it be something a little nicer, please?"

"What?" She turned it back around and studied it. "Oh, okay."

Angela got another piece of red paper—stepping on only one book this time—and wrote something else. She held up her new sign:

Be quiet please!!!

"All right." I nodded. "Not bad. Here, I'll go hang it on the refrigerator. No, wait … why don't you draw a picture on the other side first? That way the refrigerator doesn't have to be constantly yelling at all of us to be quiet."

"Sure." Angela looked deep in concentration for a moment before happily announcing, "I know. I'll draw a ballerina, a mermaid, and a unicorn all having a tea party."

"Perfect. Now, while you work on that I need to go take care of something." Before I lose my nerve, I thought.

I headed back upstairs and sat down at the kitchen table. I had my phone and the list of phone numbers I'd made earlier.

The websites that came up during my Google search for local wedding pianists were more than a little intimidating. There were photos of male pianists wearing tuxedos and female pianists wearing evening gowns with long, flowing hair cascading down past their shoulders. The bios described masters degrees in piano performance, years of studying music in Europe, and even performances for former presidents. Everybody looked impeccably polished. And they all had an air of importance about them.

Not one of them looked like they'd spent their morning as I had—cleaning various Goldfish crackers, Lego pieces, a total of twenty-seven cents in coins, a plastic fork, and six Froot Loops out from under the couch cushions. Then, of course, I worked on creative ways to get two blobs of jelly out of the living room carpet.

I briefly considered just sending emails, but I knew I couldn't be a coward. I had to suck it up and actually make the calls. I needed to learn something about how to handle a phone inquiry. I tried to convince myself that it was really no big deal. I would just ask for a quote, say thank you, and move on to the next person on my list. They would have no reason to suspect anything strange. Maybe I would even get lucky and get their voice mail.

As I was about to call Bob McMillan, the first person on my list, it struck me that speaking to another female seemed a little less intimating to start. So I skipped to the second name, Kathie Goldsby. I dialed her number and tried to keep my hands and voice steady.

"Hello," I said when she answered. "I'd like to know how much you charge to play for a wedding."

"Congratulations!" said a smooth voice on the other end of the line. "Are you the bride, or a friend or relative calling on her behalf?"

I hadn't expected that. "Uh … yes, I'm the bride." I cleared my throat. "Yup. That's me. In love and getting married."

"That's wonderful, congratulations again," said Kathie. "Are you wanting live piano music for the ceremony, cocktail hour, reception, or all three?"

Oh crap. I didn't realize there would be questions. "All three," I said and quickly added, "but I'd like to have them all priced separately. So we can … um, decide which options we can afford."

"Of course." She tapped her fingers on computer keys. "Now, where will your wedding be located?"

"Yeah, uh … that." I coughed. Clearly, I hadn't thought this through either. "Yes. Um …" I was frantically trying to think. Where should I tell her the wedding is? I don't even know the names of many wedding venues in town yet. I know! What was the name of the place where Emily said she was getting married when she called me? Um … something like … "Twin Pines Country Club!" I blurted out.

"Twin Pines Country Club?" Kathie paused. "I'm not familiar with that. Is it in town?"

"Uh … yes?" I squeaked.

"Hmm, Twin Pines … oh! Do you mean Twin *Lakes* Country Club?"

"Yes!" I laughed nervously. "Sorry about that. How silly of me. I can't even remember where my own wedding is!" I laughed again. "There's just too much information

to keep track of, you know, planning a wedding and all."
I cleared my throat. Would this phone call ever be over?

"Oh, I understand," she said. "It can be pretty
overwhelming. Now, will the cocktail hour and reception
both be held at Twin Lakes?"

"Yup, all at the same place." I exhaled in relief. Okay,
the hard part was over.

"And what is the date of your wedding?"

AARRRGH!!! "May," I said quickly. "May …
fifteenth." That sounded nice and wedding-like.

"This coming May?" she asked.

"Uh … sure."

I heard the clicking of computer keys, then a pause.

"You're getting married on a Thursday?" Kathie asked.

Uh-oh. Was I? Did people even do that? Did I just give
myself away? Was the jig up? "Um … uh … did I say May
fifteenth?" I forced a laugh that sounded more like a
whimper. "My goodness, all the stress of being a bride is
getting me all mixed up. I meant the thirteenth … uh …
no, I mean, uh … seventeenth … or … well, whatever
that Saturday is."

"May seventeenth?"

"Yes! Saturday, May seventeenth. Yes. That's the day
I'm getting married. Me. The bride. Getting married at
Twin, uh … Lakes Country Club." I hesitated. "It is Twin
Lakes, right?"

"Yes, Twin Lakes." Kathie sounded a little puzzled.
"Okay, then. I'm available that day and would love to play
for your wedding."

"Great! So how much do you charge?"

"Well, first let me tell you a little more about what I
offer," she said. "The ceremony package includes thirty

minutes of prelude music while your guests are arriving, and …"

As she described her packages, I hurriedly began taking notes.

"Now, how many guests are you expecting?" she asked.

I slapped my palm against my forehead. What was with this woman? Did she not know what she charged? Couldn't she just answer the stupid question? And how was the number of guests going to make any difference anyway? What, did she charge per person?

"Um, uh … a hundred guests," I said.

"All right." She was tapping away on her keyboard again. "And are you planning on having any other instrumentalists, or a soloist?"

"Nope. Just piano. Nothing else."

Why couldn't she just tell me a *price*! Just name a *number*! Was that so difficult?

"And what type of musical selections are you and your fiancé considering? Are you picturing traditional style music, or did you have something more modern in mind?"

"Both," I said. "Either. Whatever. Anything!" AARRRGH!!!

"And did you have any special songs that you wanted to request? For example, any songs that have significant meaning for the two of you?"

"Nope. No special songs," I snapped. "Uh … I mean … what I mean is … any song would have meaning. Anything at all. Because … it's our special day. To get married at Twin Pines, I mean, Lakes. No, wait … yes. Twin Lakes! On Saturday, May sixteenth."

There was a pause. "You mean Saturday, May seventeenth?"

"Right. Whatever. So how much would it be? Because we need to know right away if it fits into our budget."

"Of course. I offer a special package for the ceremony, cocktail hour, and reception which is a better deal than if you decide to go with one or two of those. The package deal is only …"

I scribbled down all the numbers. "Great! Well, thanks. I'll be in touch."

"Wait! I never got your name."

"Uh … my name?" I repeated. "My name is … Mary. Mary …" I desperately glanced around the room. "Doorknob." I winced as soon as I said it. What the heck kind of name was that?

"Mary Doorknob?"

"Yup. That's me. Thank you!" I hung up and took a deep breath. Who knew this would be so painful?

Before I had a chance to chicken out, I immediately dialed the second number on my list. Hopefully this next pianist would just give me a quote without asking so many questions.

"Hello, I'd like to know how much you charge to play for a wedding," I said.

Silence.

"Didn't you just call me?" said a smooth female voice.

My eyes darted down to the list of phone numbers. I remembered that I'd skipped the first number and started with the second number. I froze. Oh crap.

"So soll-ee," I said in a high-pitched voice. "I zeenk I have zee wrong number."

I hung up and ferociously scribbled out the phone number I'd just called. Then I tossed my pencil and pad of paper across the table and headed to the freezer.

I needed to calm my nerves with a bowl of mocha almond fudge ice cream. Then I would try again.

Four

"Hey, come on in!" said my friend Stephanie Porter as she opened her front door. "We were just mummifying a chicken."

"Doing what to a chicken?" I asked.

Danny and Angela ran past me. They headed to the Porter's playroom with Trevor and Ashley, Stephanie's kids. I followed Stephanie through her living room—books were strewn all over the couches, floor, and coffee table—and into her kitchen.

"Mummifying a chicken." Stephanie brushed the debris off the kitchen counter into the trash and washed her hands. "We've been studying the ancient Egyptians. Of course, the chicken won't actually be mummified for a few weeks. Today we just scooped out the innards and coated everything in salt and cinnamon. See?" She smiled as she held up a pan containing a raw chicken smothered with salt inside a Ziploc bag. There were three baby food jars around the edge of the pan.

"What's in the jars?"

"The innards. The ancient Egyptians mummified the intestines and other organs in Canopic jars, so we figured we'd do that too."

"Lovely." I did my usual routine at Stephanie's house which was grabbing a diet soda out of the fridge, hopping up on one of the stools at her kitchen island, and gently pushing aside whatever happened to be on the counter. Today it was a bin of markers, a half-completed math worksheet, and three containers of Play-Doh—two of them without a lid.

Stephanie and I met through a play group, back in the days when Danny and Stephanie's son Trevor were both learning to walk. Between the facts that Stephanie was homeschooling her kids and she used to be an elementary art teacher … well, let's just say that I was used to quite interesting things often going on at her house.

"So," Stephanie said, taking a big bag out of her refrigerator crisper drawer and carrying it over to the counter, "how's the wedding piano business going?"

Not surprisingly, after Steve, Stephanie was the first person I'd told about my new venture. Without the slightest hesitation, she'd said she thought it was a fantastic idea and that it was about time I got over the whole incident in college. I guess nothing sounds ridiculous when your days are filled with scooping out raw chicken innards and putting them into baby food jars for fun.

"Well, I'm working on it," I said. "So far, I've got my listing with Wedding Wild, I found a freelancer who helped me get a simple website up, and I practice the piano for about an hour every day while the kids are in school."

Stephanie put a cabbage on the cutting board and started hacking at it with a butcher knife.

"What are you making?" I asked.

"We're boiling red cabbage for tomorrow's science experiment." Stephanie continued whacking away. "You use the cabbage juice as a pH indicator."

"Oh, right." I wasn't sure I even knew what a pH indicator was.

"We'll use the juice to test different items around the house, to see if they're an acid or base." Stephanie put down the butcher knife. "What you need is a good marketing strategy. Something unique, something that would reach a lot of people. Hmm …" She picked the knife up with a dramatic flair and went back to furiously hacking up the cabbage, as if the intensity would cause a brilliant idea to form in her mind. After about twenty whacks, she whirled around toward me. "I know. This is perfect!"

I flinched at the edge of her butcher knife which was pointing at me.

"Oh, sorry." Stephanie looked at her hand and set the knife down on the cutting board. "Okay!" She clasped her hands. "Are you ready?"

I nodded.

She pulled up the stool across from me, sat down, and leaned forward. "Okay, get this. You bring your whole family to a baseball game, or a football game, or whatever, and every time the crowd jumps up and cheers, or does a wave or something, all four of you jump up and throw a bunch of your business cards in the air like confetti!" She leaped off the stool and tossed up her hands, lowered them, and grinned at me. "Isn't that great? You'll get your business card everywhere in one afternoon, and it'll be fun too." She clutched my arm. "Hey, can we come too? That'll give you five more people to throw cards! We'll throw them in one direction and you guys can throw them in the other direction."

"Yeah, I'm sure the kids would love that," I muttered. "But how, exactly, will that get me any business?"

"Hundreds of people in town will catch a copy of your business card," Stephanie said excitedly. "They'll say, hey, wow, this person plays the piano for weddings! And they'll know how to contact you."

I thought for a minute. "Or …" I said slowly, "most of the cards will end up between the bleachers and the only person who will even see them is whoever sweeps the floor at the end of the night … after the cards are soggy with sloshed beer and have been stepped on twenty-five times. And anyway, isn't that littering?"

"Oh yeah." Stephanie sounded disappointed. "I hadn't thought of that." She put the knife in the sink and turned back to me. "You know what would be a better idea? Meet some wedding planners, make a good impression. When a bride wants a wedding pianist, who do you think is going to help her find one?"

Of course. That was a great idea. "How would I find them?"

She shrugged. "I don't know. There must be some place where wedding planners all hang out. Check it out online. There's gotta be some local meetings or something for people in the wedding business."

It didn't sound like such a great idea anymore. "You mean I should *go* to a meeting? Just show up at a roomful of strangers. I don't know …"

Stephanie shrugged again. "You gotta do what you gotta do." A line of petri dishes near the sink caught her attention. "Oh, look! The germs are finally growing."

"What?"

"That's the science project we started last week." She pointed at the little dishes. "We're growing germs."

"Germs? What kind of germs?"

"See, look, they're all labeled." Stephanie brought them over to the counter and set them in front of me. "We scraped the samples and put them in these petri dishes on Monday. After seven days we'll see which germs grew the fastest, and then we'll make a bar graph."

I wrinkled my nose. "And you do all this in the kitchen?"

She didn't hear me.

"Oh, look! The sample we scraped from between Katie's toes is winning." Stephanie grinned at me. "That's surprising, isn't it? You'd think the sample from inside the toilet rim would have the most germs, but ..." She studied the dishes again. "No, wait. The sample from between her toes and the one from inside her cheek are winning! Who would have thought?"

"Not me," I mumbled.

She saw the look on my face. "Oh, don't worry. The germs are sealed inside the petri dishes."

I nodded. Somehow, that didn't make me any more enthusiastic about the experiment.

I heard the sound of footsteps on the stairs. Angela and Katie came running into the kitchen.

"Miss Heather," said Katie, "Angela has a bug in her hair!"

"A bug in her hair?" I said. "What do you mean? Were you guys playing outside?"

"Look, Katie." Stephanie beckoned her over to the petri dishes. "Your germs are growing!"

"Really?" Katie rushed over to the counter. "Oh wow, the toe germs are winning!"

"And the germs from your mouth," Stephanie said proudly. "I think it's a tie."

"Wait a minute," I said. "What about the bug in Angela's hair?" I stood up and brushed my fingers through the ends of Angela's curly hair. "What bug?"

"Katie said she saw a bug when she was braiding my hair," said Angela. "Do you see it Mommy?"

"No." I lifted her hair up at different angles. "What, was it like a bumblebee or something? Do you think it flew away?"

"No, not on the ends of her hair." Katie walked over to us. "It was more on her head."

"Her head?" I said, getting nervous. "You mean her scalp?"

"Yeah." Katie started rooting through the top of Angela's hair. "I was braiding her hair, and … oh, here it is." She pointed. "See?"

I looked closely. There was a tiny reddish-brown bug in Angela's hair. "Oh no!" I shrieked. "Is that what I think it is?"

"Wait. What is it?" Angela asked.

Stephanie came over and inspected the top of Angela's head. "Ooh, I think that might be lice. Katie, run and get the laptop for me. Oh, and tell the boys to come up."

Katie hurried out of the room.

"What's lice?" Angela asked, scratching her head.

"Lice," I said grimly, "are bugs that lay eggs in people's hair."

"Eww!" she yelled.

Danny and Trevor came running into the kitchen. Katie followed them and handed her mother a laptop.

"What's up?" Trevor asked.

"We're going to learn about lice," Stephanie announced. She placed the laptop on the counter, opened it, and began typing. "There! Here's a photo of one." She started reading aloud. "Head lice are tiny, wingless, parasitic insects that live and feed on blood from the scalp. One louse can lay as many as a hundred eggs. A louse can live up to thirty days on a human scalp, and up to two days without food or nutrition. The nits, eggs, can live up to two weeks without nutrition but are susceptible to temperature."

"Eww!" Angela yelled again. "That's what's on my head?" She frantically rubbed her head with her fingertips.

Danny's eyes lit up. "That mutant bug is in Angela's hair? Where?" He ran over to her and started digging through her hair.

"Get off me!" Angela screamed, giving him a shove.

"It's not that big, Danny," said Stephanie. "The picture is magnified." She typed some more and then read from the screen. "A female head louse, that's the singular form of lice, produces about four to six eggs per day. Since there is sometimes no visible sign of infestation initially, there can be hundreds of head lice on one person's head, depending on how long they have been infected. Oh, and here's a true or false question for everybody." Stephanie turned toward the kids. "Lice is caused by not washing your hair often enough. True or false?"

"True!" Trevor bellowed.

"No, Trevor," Stephanie said, "that's actually false. It says here that lice are not signs of unwashed hair or poor hygiene. In fact, they thrive in clean hair." She turned to

Katie. "Katie, can you get that bug out of Angela's hair?" Stephanie rushed over to the cabinets. "We can put it in … this." She pulled out a small Tupperware container. "Trevor, go down to the playroom and bring us the magnifying glass. It's on the brown shelf by the Snap Circuits Kit."

"Here Mom, I've got it." Katie walked over to Stephanie with her fingers carefully pinched together as Trevor ran out of the room.

"Wait, so we're going to *study* the louse?" I said.

"Sure, why not?" said Stephanie. "Okay everybody, gather around."

Trevor returned with the magnifying glass.

"Can anyone tell me how many legs it has?" Stephanie asked.

Danny bobbed his index finger a few times and then yelled, "Six!"

"Very good, Danny!" Stephanie smiled at him.

Danny beamed.

"Can I hold the magnifying glass?" Angela asked.

"Sure." Stephanie handed it to her and stepped out of the way.

"Wow," said Trevor, leaning over to see. "It's got, like, ridges."

"And you can see its eyes!" Danny said. "Cool!"

"Eww!" Angela yelled again.

Stephanie clapped her hands. "Oh, I know!" She grabbed a pair of scissors off the counter and started running her fingers carefully through Angela's hair. "Angela, if you don't mind, I'm going to snip a little piece of hair that has a nit … ah! Here we go!" She clipped a strand of hair off Angela's head and put it inside the

Tupperware next to the louse. "What does the nit look like under the magnifying glass?"

"Here Angela, let me hold the magnifying glass!" Katie snatched it from her. "Oh wow, it looks like it's stuck to the hair!"

"So, how would you describe the shape and color?" Stephanie asked.

"It's kinda like … like a seed," said Trevor, squinting.

"Yeah," Katie said. "It's a little pointy on one end, and bumpy on the other."

"So does anyone have any questions about lice?" asked Stephanie.

"Yeah, I have one," I said, waving my hand. "How do we get *rid* of all of them?"

"Hmm." Stephanie went back to her laptop. "Let's see … head lice are killed with over the counter medicines applied to the scalp, followed by careful removal of all nits with a special lice comb."

"Okay, kids," I sighed, "party's over. We've got to head to the drug store and then go straight home."

The kids completely ignored me and continued studying their specimens.

"Of course," said Stephanie, "you could always call the Lice Lady. But she is kind of expensive."

"The Lice Lady?" I echoed.

"Yeah, I've heard some of my friends talk about her." Stephanie shut the laptop. "She'll come to your house and pick out all the nits for you."

"Really?" I said. "That's someone's job?"

"Uh-huh. And from what I hear, she gets an awful lot of business."

"Well, that's very interesting, but I think we'll save our money and pick them out ourselves." I stood up, crumpled my soda can, and tossed it in the recycling bin. "Kids! Come on! We've got to head to the drug store, then go home and kill all of Angela's new little friends."

"Huh?" Angela looked startled. "What friends?"

"The lice." I sighed.

"Oh," said Angela.

"Good luck," I told Stephanie as I headed to the door with the kids trailing behind me. "I hope your kids don't have them too."

"I'll check." Stephanie's face brightened. "If they do have any, that'll give us more specimens to study. Ooh, and the kids can make some sketches in their science journals."

"Of course," I said as we walked out the door. "Have fun growing your germs."

"We will!" she called after us.

* * *

Two hours later Danny, Angela, and I were all piled in the kids' bathroom. I'd checked Danny and found some nits in his hair as well.

He was sitting on the edge of the tub with a towel around his neck and chemicals in his hair. Angela was sitting cross-legged on the floor in front of the toilet as I tugged at her hair with the lice comb.

"Ewww, this stuff stinks!" Danny whined. "How much longer?"

I looked at the timer. "Only two minutes until we wash it out."

"It's getting in my eyes!" he yowled.

"Wipe them with the end of your towel." I gave him a quick glance before turning back to Angela's hair. "Ugh! Now I lost my place." I flipped a few strands of Angela's hair back and forth. "Did I already do this section?"

"How much longer?" Danny moaned.

I heard the garage door open.

Steve appeared in the bathroom doorway a couple minutes later. "Hey, what's up?"

"They both have lice." I looked at him grimly. "Angela, stay still! This is difficult enough without you moving your head around."

"Are you almost done?" she whined.

"Almost done? I'm not even close. I'm not even halfway."

The timer went off.

"Rinse it off! Rinse it off!" Danny yelled.

"Hang on," I said, sliding two more dead bugs off the comb with a tissue.

"Uh … is there anything I can do to help?" Steve looked like he dreaded hearing the answer.

I set down the comb, leaned toward the tub, and turned on the water. "Yes. Go get your razor and shave both kids' heads."

"Hey!" Angela shrieked.

"Mommy's just kidding," said Steve.

"Just barely." I started scrubbing Danny's head. When I was finished, I wrapped it with the towel. "Just … sit here for a minute. Maybe Daddy can start working on your hair now."

"What about you?" Steve asked.

"What about me?" I snapped, plopping back to my seat on the toilet and snatching the lice comb. "I already have plenty to do! I've been working on Angela's hair for over an hour, and I still haven't even …"

"Ow!" Angela squealed. "Mommy, you're hurting me!"

"Sorry," I muttered, relaxing my grip on her hair.

"No," said Steve. "I mean, what about you? Do you have lice too?"

The comb stopped in mid-air as I looked at him. "What? What are you talking about? Adults don't get lice."

Steve shrugged as he walked toward me. "Why not? We have hair too. You always lie down next to the kids when you read them their bedtime stories. Who knows, maybe something crawled in your hair then." He flipped my hair around for a few seconds. "I don't see any bugs. You have a little dandruff though."

"Dandruff?" I tensed up. "Does … does it look like little seeds?"

Steve fingered my hair a little more slowly. "Kind of." He paused and pulled at a strand. "And it won't slide off either. It's almost like it's stuck to your hair or something."

"NOOOO!!" I buried my head in my hands. "Those are lice eggs!"

"So Mom has bugs too?" Danny leaped up from his spot on the tub. "Cool!"

"What about Daddy?" Angela asked.

Steve and I exchanged glances. We switched places without saying a word. The kids joined me in rummaging through their father's hair.

It occurred to me that some families spend their evenings eating popcorn and watching a Disney movie, while other families sit around the kitchen table playing a game of Uno or Apples to Apples Junior. We, on the other hand, had family bonding time as we gathered together in the bathroom picking the bugs out of each others' hair.

"Anything?" Steve asked.

"Here's a couple little white things," said Angela.

I looked closely where her fingers were and exhaled loudly. "I cannot *believe* this."

"I'm guessing that's a yes," Steve said.

"So we're all growing bugs in our heads?" said Danny, happily digging through Steve's hair. "That is so cool!"

"Yeah, it's just lovely." I turned around and headed out of the bathroom.

"Hey, where are you going?" asked Steve.

"I'm officially done," I said over my shoulder. "I'm calling the Lice Lady."

I got Crystal the Lice Lady on the phone. She informed me of a few things.

First, the money and time I'd spent treating Danny and Angela had been a complete waste. Apparently, the drug store lice treatments don't even work because lice have built up resistance to them over the years.

Second, we had to drench everybody's hair in olive oil and cover our heads with shower caps. The idea was that all the little bugs would suffocate to death while we slept on greasy pillows that night.

Third—well, after spending over half an hour scrubbing gobs of oil out of everybody's hair—Crystal the Lice Lady would come over. She would pick every single nit and louse corpse off all four of our heads.

And fourth, I would have to pay Crystal the Lice Lady a lot of money that we really didn't have.

When she was finished with us, I spent the afternoon vacuuming couch cushions, washing two loads of bed sheets in hot water, and running Bunny-Bun and some of the other popular stuffed animals through the dryer.

I kept telling myself that it would be okay. Soon, I would be getting some wedding jobs and finally start bringing in some money. And it would all be okay.

At least I really hoped so.

Five

As much as I hated to admit it, Stephanie was right. I had to get out there and meet other wedding professionals.

I did a Google search and found a group called The Madison Wedding and Event Professionals. They were hosting a lunch and learn in a couple weeks.

* * *

The day of the lunch and learn I put on a skirt and high heels for the first time in almost two years. Then I headed off to the Midtown Terrace.

I pushed open the glass doors and signed in at the registration desk in the front lobby. I walked into the ballroom and lurked around the edge, taking it all in. A DJ was set up against the back wall, and people—LOTS of people—were scattered around the room in clusters, chatting.

Everyone seemed to know each other. As far as I could tell, I was the only person who was alone, wandering around aimlessly.

I finally made my way to the bartender in the back corner, partly because it gave me something to do, and partly because I thought I might feel more comfortable if I had a drink in one hand. I got a glass of wine, but unfortunately, it didn't really help.

What exactly was I supposed to do? Most people were standing in groups of three or four. I couldn't just butt into their conversations. And even if I did, what could I say?

I continued meandering around the room until I finally saw another woman who was alone. Aha, here was my chance! I took a few steps in her direction, thinking of the best way to introduce myself.

Before I got to her, a woman wearing gold hoop earrings and a red scarf that perfectly matched her boots came bouncing out of nowhere. "Julie!" she said, squealing and giving the woman who was previously alone a big hug. "I saw you were featured in *Bridal Style*. Congratulations!"

I pivoted and kept walking. This must be what it feels like to be a guy in a singles bar, I thought.

By the time I'd finished circling the room people were starting to migrate to seats, thankfully. I headed toward the nearest table and sat down.

A dark-haired woman with glasses was in the seat next to me. She looked up and smiled. "Hi!"

"Hi," I said, relieved to finally introduce myself to someone. "I'm Heather. This is my first time here."

"Welcome, Heather!" she said. "You'll love it. They get some really great speakers, and the food is always fantastic too." She plucked a business card off a little stack she had on the table and handed it to me. "I'm Elizabeth Kirkpatrick, the catering and sales director at the West End Country Club."

"Nice to meet you, Elizabeth." I reached into my purse and pulled my business cards out of a zippered compartment. "I'm a musician. I play the piano."

Her eyes lit up as she took my card. "Great! We could use some musicians to add to our preferred vendor list. Sometimes brides ask for referrals and I don't have any names to give them."

I almost couldn't believe what I was hearing. A catering and sales director at a country club who *needs* names of musician she can refer to her clients? Yes!

"So," said Elizabeth, setting my card down next to her stack, "do you have your own keyboard that you bring with you?"

Nooo!! "Uh …" Could I get away with lying? "Well …" I guess not. "No. No, I don't."

"Oh." Elizabeth's smile faded. "Oh. That's too bad. We don't have a piano at the country club, so we would need any musicians to have their own instruments." She shifted her weight slightly and started talking to the person sitting on the other side of her.

Aargh!!

Of course I needed a portable keyboard. Had I been thinking that every building in the world was furnished with a nice piano? And even if they all were, what about outdoor weddings? I felt so stupid I could slap myself.

I was in the middle of wondering what it would cost to buy a full-sized keyboard, a decent-looking stand, and a traveling case when I heard an announcement.

"Welcome to the Midtown Terrace, and to today's lunch and learn!" said a woman at the front of the room.

She had a ton of dark wavy hair, a short skirt, long legs, and the spikiest high heels I'd ever seen.

"I'm Erica Cantrell, president of Madison Wedding and Event Professionals, as well as the owner of Magical Moments Event Planning." She paused for a moment to let that sink in as she flashed a huge smile. "As you probably know, we still have plenty of booths available for our semiannual Beautiful Bridal Bazaar which is next month. As you know, this is the largest bridal show in the entire Madison area and surrounding counties. We're expecting six hundred brides to attend, so you want to make sure you get your chance to meet them face to face. In the middle of your tables you'll find cards with more information about the Bazaar and how to register."

A bridal show—of course! If I registered for this show and got to meet even a few of those six hundred brides, I'd be sure to book a bunch of weddings. I leaned forward and plucked one of the glossy cards off the center of the table.

Taking a sip of my wine, I read about the event that would be my ticket to success … until I saw the price and nearly choked. I flipped the card over, desperately hoping that maybe the number was some sort of group rate and the *real price* was somewhere on the back. No. That was the real price.

As waiters came around the tables with plates of chicken and asparagus, Erica Cantrell—president of Madison Wedding and Event Professionals, as well as the owner of Magical Moments Event Planning—announced the speaker. I stared vaguely in the speaker's direction.

I couldn't stop reading and rereading the card in my hand, trying to decide if we could afford the hefty price tag. It was a ton of money that we didn't have, especially now that I had to buy a keyboard on top on everything else.

But what were my options? I couldn't just sit around and hope people would find me. And I certainly wasn't going to give up before I'd even started. Steve and I had agreed that if I was going to do this, I should do it right. But still …

As I debated my dilemma more than I listened to the speaker's advice about building an email list, I noticed Erica Cantrell—president of Madison Wedding and Event Professionals, as well as the owner of Magical Moments Event Planning—several tables away. She leaned toward the person next to her, whispered something, then laughed silently as she tossed back her cascading locks.

Wait a minute. Maybe I didn't have to spend a fortune on advertising, at least not right away. Instead of spending hundreds of dollars on a bridal show, why couldn't I first try some strategic networking? What if I could somehow say something to Erica Cantrell—president of Madison Wedding and Event Professionals, as well as the owner of Magical Moments Event Planning—that would completely win her over, cause her to remember the charming strawberry-blond piano player, and inspire her to refer me not only to her many brides, but also to her slew of wedding vendor friends?

The waiters came around with little plates of strawberry shortcake as we applauded the speaker. I was quite proud of my clever, and inexpensive, plan. All I had to do was come up with something brilliant to say while I had dessert …

Wait. Erica was standing up, slinging a black purse over her shoulder. She was leaving *right now.*

I snatched my business cards off the table, jammed them in my purse, and nearly tipped over my chair as I leaped to my feet. My purse thumped across my back as I hurried across the room as fast as I could in heels.

It wasn't fast enough. Erica disappeared. There were still three tables between me and the ballroom door, but I was determined not to give up. I rushed past the tables, through the lobby, and out the front door.

Erica was chatting with a woman with straight blond hair as they walked across the parking lot. I was running out of time. Any minute now she would get in her car and drive away, and I would have missed any chance to …

"Excuse me!" I blurted out as I scurried across the parking lot.

Erica and the blond woman glanced over their shoulders.

At that very moment, I tripped and went flying forward. I frenetically took several probably ridiculous-looking steps, but at least they kept me from landing face down on the pavement.

"Ahem," I said, straightening up and smoothing my hair.

Erica and her friend turned completely around to face me. I thought I saw them exchange amused looks.

"Are you okay?" the blond asked.

"Yes, I'm fine," I said, trying to catch up to them. "I …" My voice trailed off as I realized that I'd never, in fact, figured out what I should say. "I … I just wanted to introduce myself. And … and give you my card." I started digging through my purse but I couldn't find my business cards. Where did they go?

"You can mail it to me," Erica said, turning away.

"No … no, wait!" I practically screeched as I frantically rooted through my bag. "It's right here. Hang on … it's … aha!" I pulled out one of my business cards and waved it in the air. I held it toward Erica, horrified to see that not only was it bent on one side, but there were two streaks of orange crayon across the front.

Erica looked at it and smirked. "You can mail it to me."

"Nice to meet you," the blond called over her shoulder as they walked away.

I sighed as I watched them cross the parking lot. Then I crumpled up the ruined business card and stuffed it in my pocket as I walked toward the car.

Well, that plan didn't exactly work. If I wanted anything to start happening, I'd probably have to fork out the money for the bridal show after all.

We could come up with the money. We'd just have to cut back in some other ways. Like …. well, maybe like … like …

As I sat down in the car and put the key in the ignition, a thought hit me. My hand froze.

No.

Not that!

Of course, maybe desperate times call for desperate measures.

Six

"We are going to learn how to cook," I announced to the kids the next day when they got home from school.

"Cool," said Danny. "You're going to show us how to make hot dogs?"

"What? No. We're going to learn to cook."

"Oh, are we going to make those chicken pot pies we keep in the freezer?" asked Angela, her eyes lighting up. "I love those!"

"No! We're going to learn how to really cook. Cooking that involves things like chopping and sautéing and using things like peelers, and graters, and … and whisks."

"So, what are we making?" Danny seemed suspicious.

"We're starting by making a lemon meringue pie for dessert," I said, slipping an apron over my head and tying it behind me. "Then, while that chills, we'll make lasagna and garlic bread."

Angela and I put our hair into ponytails and we all washed our hands. Then we gathered around the kitchen table. I'd already set up a mixing bowl and the first few ingredients we needed for the pie.

"Okay, now the first thing we need to do is separate an egg because we need the egg white, but not the yolk," I explained. I didn't know how to make mashed potatoes or roast a chicken, but I did remember being shown how to separate an egg in my seventh grade home ec class. I was pretty pleased with myself for knowing how to do this. In fact, it was probably the reason I chose to start with a lemon meringue pie. "So here's what you do. You crack the egg and sort of drop the yolk back and forth from one half of the shell to the other while …" The yolk slid out of the shell and plopped right into the center of the bowl.

"Like that?" Danny asked.

"Uh … no." I dumped the yolk into the sink and rinsed the bowl. "Here, we'll try again." I cracked another egg and carefully slipped the yolk back and forth between the two pieces of broken shell. We all watched as a tiny yellow stream trickled into the bowl.

"Isn't that yolk?" Angela asked, pointing to the bowl.

"Yes. Yes, it is." I picked up the bowl and rinsed it out again. This looked a lot easier when my home ec teacher demonstrated how to do it.

Four eggs later, I had the three egg whites I needed for the meringue—almost. The tiniest speck of yolk had crept in, but I scooped most of it out with a spoon and figured it would be good enough. It would have to be. I was out of eggs.

Danny added the vanilla and Angela added the cream of tartar. I had no idea what it was, but I'd bought some that morning.

"Okay," I said, checking the recipe and plugging in the mixer. "Now we're supposed to beat it for about a minute, or until soft peaks form."

The three of us watched as the mixer hummed. Two minutes later there were still no peaks, soft or otherwise.

"Isn't it supposed to do something?" Angela asked over the sound of the mixer.

I frowned. "Maybe it just needs a little more time."

Four minutes later the mixer was still going, but nothing had changed. The kids were starting to get glazed looks in their eyes.

"Are we done learning how to cook yet?" Danny asked, looking around. "This is boring."

"I'm sure something will happen any second now," I said, silently pleading with the egg mixture to wake up and begin peaking already. "Look, I think right there it might be … no, I guess not." The beaters continued churning. "Okay, but I swear any second now … any second … just wait … just wait … just … just … eh, forget it." I switched off the mixer in disgust and shoved the bowl of badly behaving egg whites out of the way.

"Are we going to have to order a pizza?" Danny looked hopeful.

"Of course not. That was just the dessert. We'll worry about that later. Right now we're going to make the lasagna." I flipped to the tab I'd marked in my cookbook. "Okay, while I clear this stuff out of the way, Angela, you go to the fridge and get out the white carton of ricotta cheese and two …"

Eggs. I needed two eggs to make the lasagna and I'd just used all the eggs. Oh crap.

I was nearly in a tizzy. There was no way I could come up with two eggs, short of stopping everything we were doing and dragging the kids to the store. I definitely didn't want to go back to the store, especially since I'd already spent way too much time there that morning, wandering around trying to figure out what things like fennel and cornstarch are, and where, exactly, I could find them.

"Two what?" Angela asked, fumbling around in the fridge.

"Never mind." I sighed. "Just the ricotta cheese."

Angela took a plastic tub out of the refrigerator and held it up. She looked at me questioningly.

"Right, that's it." I handed her a measuring cup. "Now fill this up and dump it in that bowl."

"What do I get to do?" Danny asked.

I looked around, still distracted by my egg deficiency dilemma. "You get to take out the lasagna pan. It's in that cabinet down there."

I pulled the bowl of would-never-be meringue toward me. Since there was little hope of it becoming a pie at this point, I might as well use it for the lasagna … right?

I scooped up a little bit in a spoon and contemplated. Then I splashed a few spoonfuls of it in the bowl with the ricotta cheese and began to stir. I poured in a little more, just to be sure. I looked at the bowl of egg whites again. Eh, that must be close enough to two eggs, I thought. I dumped all the egg mixture in with the ricotta cheese and began stirring, proud of myself.

"Look," I said to Angela, "the egg whites didn't go to waste after all."

"But Mommy," she said, "wasn't there other stuff mixed in with the eggs?"

Angela wasn't as impressed with her mother's brilliance as I'd hoped. I stopped stirring.

Aargh!!! I'd totally forgotten that we'd added vanilla and cream of tartar to the egg whites. Does it matter? Is it going to ruin the lasagna? What is cream of tartar anyway? What the heck does it even do?

"Yes … well," I said, slowly resuming my stirring, "those things will make our lasagna even better. The extra ingredients will give it a, uh, creamier and richer texture."

I didn't have the slightest idea if that was true. For all I knew it would cause some chemical reaction that could make the entire thing explode. We would just have to risk it.

"Which one is the zonna pan?" Danny asked.

I looked down. Danny was sitting on the floor surrounded by skillets, muffin tins, a loaf pan, a frying pan, two different sized baking pans, and a Bundt cake pan. I didn't even realize we owned all that stuff.

"Sorry Danny, I should've been more specific. It's this big rectangular one … oh, and I'm going to need this skillet too. Can you put all the others away?"

I turned back to the counter. Angela had discovered the unopened package of ground beef. She was poking her index finger into it.

"Eww, no, Angela! Let me have that." I tore the plastic off, dumped the meat into the skillet, and turned on the heat. "Okay, now we … aarrrgh!! I'm supposed to cook the meat with a chopped onion!" I snapped off the heat, ran across the kitchen, and grabbed an onion out of the fridge.

"What can I do?" asked Angela.

"Hang on," I said, trying to keep the onion from wobbling while I cut it in half.

WHAM!! BANG!! CRASH!!

I whipped around. Danny was about to hurl a muffin tin into the cabinet. "Aaahhhh!" I yelled. "I didn't mean for you to throw everything back in there! Can't you just … why don't you …. oh, here, just let me do it." I shooed him out of the way and bent down to gather up the collection of cookware I hadn't even realized I owned.

"Can I finish cutting the onion for you?" Angela asked.

"No!" I yelled, trying to shove all the pans back in the cabinet.

"Can I?" Danny asked.

"NO!" The Bundt pan bounced back at me as if it had a mind of its own. I gave it another shove, slammed the cabinet door shut before anything else could fall out, and went back to my onion.

"This is boring," Danny whined.

I went to the pantry, grabbed cans of tomato sauce and tomato paste, and put them on the counter. "Angela, you get the can opener and open these. Danny, you can …" I looked over the recipe, "go get a bag of mozzarella cheese out of the refrigerator."

I grabbed the onion and knife and tried again. *Chop, chop, chop, chop, chop.*

"I can't get the can opener to work," said Angela.

"Is this mustard ella cheese?" Danny held up a block of Velveeta.

"No Danny, the mozzarella cheese is in a bag. Here, Angela, let me get it started." I attached the can opener to the can of tomato sauce, gave it a few twists, set it down, and went back to my onion.

Chop, chop, chop …

"So do I just dump all this in here?" Angela asked, tilting the can of tomato sauce toward the bowl of ricotta cheese and eggs—with vanilla and cream of tartar.

"No!! Wait!!" I dropped the knife and snatched the can away from her. "I'm pretty sure that goes with the meat. Here, now you can open the tomato paste."

"But I can't figure out how to use the …"

"Is this the monster ella cheese?" Danny was holding up a bag of baby carrots.

I put the knife down again and took a deep breath. "Does that look like cheese?"

Danny glanced down at the bag, then up at me. He shrugged.

"Mommy! I told you I don't know how to use the can opener!" screamed Angela.

"I'll do it." Danny dropped the carrots on the floor and stomped over to the counter.

"Wait, you need to put the … oh, never mind." I picked up the carrots and tossed them back in the fridge. The mozzarella cheese was sitting right in the middle of the top shelf. I grabbed it.

"Quit it!" Angela yelled. "She asked me, not you!"

"You don't know how to do it!" Danny screamed as he grabbed the can opener.

"Neither do you! Hey! Give that back!"

"Get away from me!"

"AAAHH!! Danny spilled the tomato sauce!" Angela shrieked.

Both kids stood paralyzed. They stared at the flowing sauce like it was some sort of mysterious and terrifying being.

"Well don't just stand there!" I yelled, shooting across the kitchen to pick up the can. I got to it in time to salvage about half. Would that work? Did I need to add some water … or maybe ketchup or something? Could I just use what I had and hope for the best?

I looked at them wearily. And in that moment of clarity, one of the great mysteries of my life was solved. I now perfectly understood why my mother had never taught me to cook.

"Okay!" I announced, clapping my hands. "Lesson's over! That's enough cooking for you guys today. Congratulations! You now know all about separating eggs and how to open cans and, uh … what mozzarella cheese looks like."

"I never even got to do anything," said Danny.

"Sure you did. You helped with the, uh … you got to, um. Good job, sweetie!" I kissed him on the top of his head. "Class dismissed."

"Come on, Danny," Angela said. "Let's go do that thing where I put you in the laundry hamper and then roll you down the hall."

"Cool!" Danny yelled as they ran out of the kitchen.

About twenty minutes later I put my first-ever homemade lasagna into the oven. And the Italian bread was on a cookie sheet—sliced, buttered, and sprinkled with garlic powder.

Wow. I'd done it! Even if it came out tasting terribly, which at this point was still a distinct possibility, I had done it. Maybe cooking wasn't really that hard after all.

I turned around and noticed the mess. Shredded cheese was on the floor and the counter. Empty cans, plastic tubs, egg shells, wads of wet, sauce-stained paper towels, and a slew of dirty utensils were scattered everywhere. And that was in addition to two dirty pots, four dirty bowls, a slimy colander, and a cutting board covered with bits of onion. There were also various blobs of grease, tomato sauce, and egg all over the counter.

Oh. Maybe this was the hard part. I grabbed a sponge and got to work cleaning up.

When the timer for the lasagna went off I'd finally gotten the kitchen to a semi-decent state. I pulled the lasagna out of the oven and set it down.

Now it was time to make the garlic bread. I read the instructions: *Place bread under broiler for three to five minutes.* I moved the oven rack to the top position—what do you know, those things are adjustable—and slid in the tray of bread.

Since we were having a nice dinner, assuming the lasagna was indeed edible, shouldn't the dining table look a little special as well? I went down the hall to the linen closet to find the red tablecloth.

I was searching through some towels when the phone rang. "Yello!" I said, snatching up the bedroom phone.

There was silence, and then a female voice said hesitantly, "Hi, my name is Susan. I wanted to speak to someone named Heather Hershey about playing the piano for my wedding."

I have got to start answering my phone differently, I thought.

"Yes, of course. I'm Heather!" I grabbed my purse off the dresser and fumbled around for my calendar. "Congratulations! What's the date of your wedding?"

"It's on April …" There was another female voice murmuring something in the background. "Hang on. Yes, I know, Mom!" Susan hissed in reply to the muffled voice. "Do you think I don't know my own wedding date? How dumb do you think I am?"

I frowned.

"Sorry about that," said Susan. "Our wedding is on April fourteenth."

I opened my calendar and checked the month of April. "Great, I'm available that day. Do you want piano music for the ceremony, cocktail hour, or reception?" See, I did learn something from calling a few other pianists.

"I think both the ceremony and cocktail hour. We'll have the DJ play for the reception downstairs in the … What? … Yes, Mom, we are having a DJ, not a live band!" Susan sighed. "Hang on," she said to me. "How many times have we gone over this?" There was a pause. "Yes, I know, but … Yes! Yes, of course I remember Tonya's wedding. I was there, wasn't I? Yes, I know, yes. I already told you, that was because Tonya and her husband are cheap and they got a cheap, crummy DJ. Didn't we already … Seriously? Seriously Mom? You're going to bring that up now? I'm on the phone!" She cleared her throat. "Just ceremony and cocktail hour," she said sweetly into the phone.

"Ohhh … kay," I said.

"We were picturing more traditional music for the ceremony, and then some more upbeat, modern songs for the cocktail hour," said Susan. The voice in the background murmured again. "Yes Mom! I was just about to say that! Would you please just … would you … Look Mom, do you want to just get on the phone yourself? … You sure? Because it sounds like you want to be in charge of this conversation." There was another pause. "Okay, well then, let me talk!"

"Uh," I said, "maybe this is a bad time? You can call me back."

"No." She sounded surprised. "Right now is fine. We also want some show tunes."

"No problem." I made a mental note to check and see if I had any.

"So how much would you charge?"

"Well, for both the ceremony and cocktail hour …"

"HEATHER!!" Steve roared from down the hall. "HEATHER?!"

70

Uh-oh. That didn't sound like Steve's typical greeting at all. Something was very, very wrong.

"Hang on just a moment, Susan." I put the phone down and ran down the hall.

An ear-piercing *Eeeeeeeeee* filled the house.

I clapped my hand over my mouth as I entered the living room. Steve was surrounded by a cloud of black smoke.

"Oh no," I gasped, running into the kitchen. "The garlic bread!"

Steve followed me, coughing. He climbed up on a chair to pluck the batteries out of the smoke alarm before yanking open the kitchen windows.

A burst of smoke shot into my face as I opened the oven door. I was barely able to breathe as I pulled out the charred solid-black remains of the bread. I heard the kids behind me.

"What's wrong?" Angela asked as she ran into the kitchen. "Is the house on fire?"

"Are the fire engines coming?" Danny hurried over to the window at the front of the house.

"Sorry to … disappoint you," I said between coughs as I scraped the cripsy black chunks into the trash and flung the possibly unsalvageable cookie sheet onto the stovetop. "No fire. … It was just a slight … cooking mishap."

Angela looked around at all the smoke. "Wow. Does this always happen when people cook?"

"So the fire engines aren't coming?" Danny still staring hopefully out the window.

"No fire engines." I grabbed a magazine out of the rack in the living room and flapped it through the smoky air. It did no good at all.

"Heather, what happened?" asked Steve.

"I was making garlic bread," I said, giving the smoke a few more swats with the magazine before I gave up and tossed the magazine back into the rack. "But then I got a phone call from a woman who wants me to play the piano at her wedding. She kept fighting with her mother while we were on the phone, and ..." I clapped my hand over my mouth again. "I'll be right back!"

I darted back down the hall and snatched the phone up from the night table. "Hello? Susan? Are you still there? Hello?" It was too late. She'd hung up. "No no no no ..."

I hit the call return button. Of course the call went straight to Susan's voice mail. No doubt she was already on the phone speaking with other pianists who were not in the process of almost burning down their houses.

"Hi Susan," I babbled to her voice mail. "It's Heather Hershey, the wedding pianist. Sorry about that. We just had a little emergency. Well, not really an emergency," I added quickly since this was probably the last word a bride wanted to hear a potential wedding vendor say. "It's just that I had some garlic bread under the broiler and I forget to set the timer and ... I mean, not that I typically forget things! I'm normally very responsible. We always file our taxes in late March, and I usually fill my gas tank before the light ever comes on. It's just that today was practically my first time ever cooking anything. I know that sounds weird, but my mother never let us do anything in the kitchen when I was a kid, and now I totally understand why because I just tried to cook with my kids and ended up practically throwing them out of the room, and, uh ... well ... well, actually, none of that is important. What is important is that I'd love to play for your wedding. So please call me back."

I hung up the phone and rolled my eyes. Oh yeah, my rambling message is really going to make her want to hire me now, I thought.

After the smoke had mostly cleared, Steve closed the windows and I dumped a bag of salad into a bowl. Finally, we sat down to dinner.

"We helped Mommy make this lasagna," Danny said proudly.

"No kidding? What did you do?" asked Steve.

Danny thought for a moment. "I got out the pan."

"You did a good job." Steve cut a slice of lasagna and put it on Danny's plate. "Very nice pan. Evenly shaped, smooth sides, and just the right size. How did you get so good at this? Did you attend the Culinary School for Proper Pan Selection?"

"No." Danny laughed.

Steve turned to me. "So what happened with the wedding job?"

I shook my head. "I don't think I'll be hearing from her again. But you know, I think it's probably just as well. Something tells me she might have been a difficult bride to work with."

I scooped some lasagna onto Angela's plate and put some on my plate. I studied it carefully. It looked normal, at least. It smelled fine. It was so much work, and I knew I'd feel so stupid if we had to dump it in the trash. Please, please don't let it taste horrible, I thought. Please, please, don't let it …

"It's good," said Steve.

"It is?" I took a bite. "It is good! I can't believe it! Do you kids like it?"

"Uh-huh," Danny grunted, shoveling some into his mouth.

Angela nodded. "We did a good job."

"I did it!" I said, laughing. "I actually did it! It worked! So you can screw up when you cook, and it still might come out okay! Ha! Who knew?"

Everybody was too busy chewing to answer.

"The bridal show is coming up next weekend," I said, "so I'll be getting wedding jobs soon. Yes!" I punched the air with my fist. "Things are finally starting to look up."

Seven

The cost of the Beautiful Bridal Bazaar didn't end with the registration fee. Not only did I order another batch of business cards, I got a hundred brochures designed and printed, I ordered a six-foot sign for the booth, and I bought a floral centerpiece to set in the middle of the table.

I'd hoped to try out my new keyboard, thinking it would be the perfect way to draw people in. However, vendors weren't allowed to play music because it could disrupt the other vendors' booths. I figured that was just as well since I would need to be able to focus on talking to people and answering questions.

I straightened my display for about the fourth time. The main doors opened and I took a deep breath and gave a big smile as people came streaming into the room.

Most of the attendees were women, although there were a few men here and there. Nearly all the men looked a little dazed, or like they were bracing themselves for a long, tiring afternoon.

The young women were eagerly looking around the room, taking everything in as they clutched the swag bags they'd received in the lobby. They would smile and nudge their friends as they pointed to things in the handout and map. Certain displays caught their attention, making their eyes light up.

As people started heading in my general direction, they looked happy and excited and ready for a day of fun. A few gave the items on my table a quick look, but they barely even slowed down as they walked right past my booth.

A cluster of women stopped at the next booth—Bridal Bubbles and Bells—without even a glance in my direction. Hmm, I thought, maybe I need to be a little more aggressive.

I stood as close to the aisle as I could without actually blocking traffic or getting run over. "Hello!" I sang, smiling so wide that it almost hurt. "Good afternoon!" I was trying my best to make eye contact with anyone.

People were flooding around the next booth. What on Earth was going on over there? What was their secret? I shuffled a few steps to the right, leaned over, and craned my neck to try to catch a glimpse of what was attracting all these people.

"Excuse me, are you the pianist?"

I spun around in the direction of the voice. A pleasant-looking middle-aged woman was eyeing me inquisitively.

"Yes. Yes, I am," I said, getting myself into my official *professional and friendly* stance. "I'm Heather Hershey." I plucked one of my brochures off the table and handed it to her.

She adjusted her glasses as she read the brochure.

"So," I said, trying to sound perky, "are you here helping your daughter plan her wedding?"

She looked up at me, surprised. "What?"

"I said, are you planning your daughter's …" my voice trailed off as her smile vanished and she cringed, "wedding?" I squeaked, guessing my mistake too late.

"It's *my* wedding," she said quietly.

"Yes … yes of course it is. I didn't mean …"

"Have a nice day," she said, flinging my brochure on the table and hurrying off.

"Wait!" I called after her. "I didn't mean that you look … I mean, there's nothing wrong with being a bride who is, uh …" I gave up. There was nothing I could say that wouldn't make this even worse.

Bridal show lesson one: Never assume anything.

People certainly weren't lining up wanting to speak with me. So why were other booths swamped? It had to be more than just the services they were offering. I mean, was everyone really dying to have paper lanterns at their wedding?

I decided that leaving my booth unattended for a few minutes to do some investigating was worth the risk. I stepped into the flow of traffic to take a little tour.

I began peeking through the crowds at the different tables. Happily Ever After Wedding Planning had a platter of cheese and crackers in the middle of their table. Let Them Eat Wedding Cake had a person sitting behind the table and another one standing in front with a tray of sample petit fours. Bride and Bouquet Floral had a blue and white basket filled with Dove Miniatures chocolates and a pretty bouquet tied on top.

No wonder people were drawn to the other booths. All the other vendors were *feeding* everybody!

I rushed to the nearest corner of the room and whipped out my cell phone.

"Hello," said Steve.

"I need your help!" I yelped. It sounded like the TV was on in the background. I turned to face the wall so I wasn't screaming into the faces of passersby. "I need you to bring food!"

"What?" Steve asked. "You're hungry?"

"No! Not for me. For my booth. No one's stopping at my booth. I need to lure them in with food."

"Hang on a minute, I can barely hear you. Danny, turn the TV down. Danny! Turn it down. Okay, what now?"

"I need food," I wailed. "Everyone else is giving away food, so nobody's even stopping to talk to me. Well, there was this one woman, but I ended up insulting her and she got upset and walked away and then …"

"You insulted someone who came up to your booth?"

"I didn't mean to insult her. Never mind, I'll explain later. Just help me figure out what to do. We spent hundreds of dollars for me to be here today, and we don't even have the money, and now I might as well have taken that money and ripped it into tiny little pieces and flushed it down the toilet because I don't have any food and no one's coming to my booth and …"

"Wait," Steve said, "just calm down, Heather. Stop talking for a minute."

I sniffled.

"So … you want me to bring you food to pass out to people?"

"Uh-huh," I whimpered.

He took a deep breath and let it out. Finally, he said, "Heather, where is this place, exactly?"

"The Waverly Center. Down past the river, off exit seventy-nine, a few miles past the airport."

"That's almost a forty minute drive. By the time I get the kids piled into the car, and we head to the store, and ..." He took another deep breath. "Look, can't you figure out some other way to get people to talk to you?"

"Maybe," I said in a small voice. He was right, of course. By the time he bought something, drove down here, and found my booth, the bridal show would practically be over.

"And ... look," he said, "try to calm down, okay? Nobody's going to want to hire you if you act like a basket case."

I cleared my throat, made one last sniff, and said, "Thanks. I'll be all right. Maybe instead of food I can ... uh ..."

"Jump on the table and start singing? That would get people's attention."

"Maybe not that," I said with a small smile. "But I'll figure out something."

"Good luck. Love you."

"Love you too."

I shut my phone off and started walking back to my booth. I turned the corner at Luminous Paper Lanterns and Parasols and headed past Dreamy Destination Weddings.

Steve is right, I thought. I had to pull myself together. I could still do this. Just because no one had stopped to talk to me yet didn't mean it was all over. Having no refreshments at my booth just meant I would have to try a little harder to get people's attention.

I returned to my booth, took a deep breath, and smiled my biggest smile. Then I said to no one in particular, "Hi,

I'm Heather! Tell me a little bit about your upcoming wedding!"

A tall woman wearing a green scarf and holding a Manila folder hesitated. She glanced at me, then my sign.

"You're what … a musician?" she asked.

I picked up a business card and brochure and held them out to her, beaming. "Yes! I play the piano for ceremonies, cocktail hours, and receptions. Classical, pop, whatever style you like."

"Oh. We're having a DJ handle all our music," she said as she walked away.

My smile faded. I set the business card and brochure back on the table. No worries, I told myself, there are lots and lots of people here. I'll just move on to the next one.

"Hi!" I called out to the sea of people, handing my business cards and brochures to anyone who would take them. "Consider live piano music for your ceremony and cocktail hour."

A guy and girl who were holding hands approached me. They looked like they were barely twenty years old.

"Hi," the girl said. "Can we talk to you for a minute? We're looking for a musician for our ceremony."

Yes! *Yes*! Finally, a real, true potential lead. Someone who is actually *looking* for a pianist.

"Certainly." I was so excited I was trying to resist the urge to bounce up and down on my toes. "Why don't you tell me a little bit about yourselves and your wedding."

"Okay," she said, looking at the guy and smiling. "I'm Brandy and this is my fiancé, Peter."

"What do you charge?" Peter asked.

"We're on a tight budget," Brandy explained. She sounded apologetic.

"Well, of course," I said, pleased with how professional I sounded. "Anybody planning a wedding has to consider their budget. Depending on what services you're looking for, my prices range from …"

"We were hoping to spend no more than fifty dollars," Peter interrupted.

"Fifty dollars?" No, wait. I must've heard him wrong. "I'm sorry. Did you say a hundred fifty dollars?"

"No," he said, giving me a bewildered look. "I said fifty dollars."

"Right … fifty dollars." I was trying my best to keep my expression completely neutral so that I wouldn't look as horrified as I felt.

"Yeah," said Brandy, "we just need someone to play for about ten minutes."

"Not even," Peter said. "Just long enough for three bridesmaids to come down the aisle, and then Brandy's entrance. So what is that … five, maybe six or seven minutes at the most?"

"Yeah, probably." Brandy shrugged.

"Yeah, so maybe even forty dollars," said Peter. "That's fair, right?"

"Well, I … I don't think …"

"Oh, and we would need you to bring and set up your own keyboard," Brandy added. "Our venue doesn't have a piano. It's a great venue though. The Rolling Hills Country Club of Belmont."

"Belmont?" I said. "What part of town is that? I'm not familiar with it."

"Oh, it's about ten miles north of Springfield," said Brandy.

"Springfield?" I asked, somewhat alarmed. "You mean you're getting married in another *state*? Springfield is over a hundred miles away."

"Uh-huh," she said. "That's where my family lives. So, does that sound like something you can do?"

I think my mouth might have been hanging open. I closed my mouth long enough to gulp while I figured out how to answer them.

"Well, I do have an extra fee for bringing my keyboard," I said. "Plus, there's a travel fee for that kind of distance."

Peter frowned for a moment, then shrugged. "Sure," he said, "that's fair. We don't mind throwing in another ten dollars. Fifty total would be fine."

They both smiled and nodded at me, as if the deal had been settled.

"No," I said slowly. "No, the fees *alone* would be fifty dollars."

"Oh." Brandy said, looking uncomfortable. She glanced at Peter for a cue.

"It's okay," he told her. "We can probably ask your aunt to do it for free, or your cousin Mary. Doesn't she know how to play the piano?"

"Oh, of course." Brandy looked relieved. "We should have thought of that in the first place. Ooh, you're so smart Peter!"

Peter looked very pleased with himself.

"Nice talking to you!" Brandy chirped, giving me a little wave with a flip of her fingers before they disappeared into the crowd.

I slowly returned her wave, which I don't think she even saw. I was watching them walk away when I heard a female voice say, "Excuse me, are you the piano player?"

"Oh, yes!" I said, snapping out of my daze.

A young woman with a blond ponytail was looking at me. Behind her was a woman wearing an emerald-green blazer. She had the thickest, waviest dark hair I'd ever seen.

Somehow, I felt like I'd seen that hair before—being tossed around proudly by the head it was attached to. Wait a minute. Was that … ? I glanced down at her feet and saw a pair of taupe patent leather stilettos. It was! It was none other than Erica Cantrell—president of Madison Wedding and Event Professionals, as well as the owner of Magical Moments Event Planning.

I hadn't wanted Erica to associate Heather Hershey wedding pianist with the bumbling idiot who almost dove face first into the parking lot the day of the lunch and learn. And fortunately, I'd been smart enough to not send her my business card.

Maybe she wouldn't remember me and this would be my second chance to make a good first impression. I stood a little straighter and nervously tucked my hair behind my ears, hoping that my dress wasn't crooked and that there wasn't any lipstick on my teeth.

"I'm Jessica," said the woman with the blond ponytail, "and this is my wedding planner, Erica."

Erica gave me a self-assured nod.

At that very moment, my left eye suddenly started to twitch and sting. Oh no! Oh no no no no no! My mascara must've flaked off and gotten trapped by my contact lens.

I sniffled and blinked a couple times. I told myself I could endure the pain. I'd just have to push through so that I could win over this bride, and more importantly, Erica. With any luck, maybe it would clear up in a minute.

"I know that I want live music for my ceremony," Jessica said, "although I haven't decided what instrument yet. We were talking about a string quartet or a harp, but then I saw your card here and thought piano might be nice too."

"Nice to meet you," I said, smiling and trying to ignore the fact that my left eyeball felt like it was on fire. "I'm Heather Hershey. Why don't you tell me a little bit about your wedding?"

"Well," said Jessica, "we're having a really romantic setup with lots of candles and flowers, so we want music that really fits that mood. You know, lots of flowing, romantic …" She peered at me. "Is something wrong?"

"Oh, just a little something in my eye. No big deal." I chuckled and dabbed the tear that was streaming down my face with my finger. "So, you want romantic music. Well, piano music would be a wonderful choice." I shot a smile at Erica who just stared at me calmly. "For example, I have many classical pieces that would …"

It felt like my entire head had turned into a set of faucets. I sniffled again. Why hadn't I packed any tissues in my purse? Why? Because I'd had no idea this was going to happen, that's why.

I debated running the back of my hand under my nose to catch the impending gush, but decided that would seem awfully gauche. Instead, I tried to stifle the coming fountain with a few more sniffles. It sounded like I was snorting.

"Excuse me." I lifted my index finger and turned my back to them as I swiped the contact lens out of my eye. I kept the contact pinched between my fingers—I'd figure out what to do with it later—as I rubbed the tears under my eye with my knuckles. I gave a few more sniffles, then turned around with a big smile. "Thank you," I said with one final sniff. "Okay, so we were talking about flowing, romantic music. I have a lot of classical music that could fit the mood, or if you're looking for songs that are a little more modern, then maybe …" My voice faded.

Jessica was giving me a strange look. "You, uh, you have a big black smudge under your eye." She tapped her finger on her cheekbone.

"Oh. Thank you." I rubbed my finger under my eye a few times. "Okay, so as I was saying, I …"

Jessica glanced uncomfortably at Erica who looked amused.

Jessica looked back at me. "It's still there."

"Heh heh …" I forced a laugh. "Well, you know how mascara can be. Hang on just a minute …"

"Maybe we should come back later." Jessica shot an uneasy look at Erica who nodded in agreement.

"No, wait! I'm fine!" I turned away from them, furtively licked my finger, and rubbed it under my eye. "There! I've got it now! I'm fine!"

"Why don't you go ahead and finish taking care of your, uh … issues," said Erica. "We know how to reach you."

"No, wait!" I whirled back around, hoping that I'd wiped the black smudge off my face rather than making it worse. "Everything's taken care of. I'd be happy to talk with you now. Candles! Flowers! Romantic music!"

"We'll call you." Erica gave me a condescending smile as she turned to go. "Let me introduce you to the harpist in the lobby," Erica said to Jessica as they walked away. "I think you'll like her. She's very professional."

AARRRGH!!!

I stood there stunned as they disappeared into the crowd. My nose was still running, my contact lens was pinched between my fingers getting dry and crispy, and the left side of my face probably looked like a tear-stained, black-smeared, scary mess. There was nothing to do but shuffle to the restroom and attempt to put my face back together.

When I returned to my booth my face looked fine, but the rest of me felt awful. Today was supposed to be the big turning point, the moment Steve and I had been waiting for, the kickoff to a wonderful career being a successful wedding musician. Instead, not only did I spend a ton of money for nothing, I'd made a total fool out of myself in front of the one person I was hoping to impress.

What was I going to do now? How long could we keep sinking money into this without having anything to show for it? Should I just quit trying? If I did, would I have to get a hideous office job where I would spend all day crunching numbers and …

"Ceremony music! That's what we forgot!" said a voice.

Two young women were approaching me.

My brain screeched to a halt and immediately switched gears. "Hi, I'm Heather!" I was as bubbly as I could possibly be.

"I'm Christine," said one of them. "My wedding is next month and when my sister and I heard about the show today we thought it would be fun to check it out and get some last-minute ideas. And I realized when I saw your sign that I totally forgot about ceremony music." She suddenly looked nervous. "Do you think you'll still be available on such short notice?"

I fought the intense urge to leap up and down the aisle while cheering and turning a few cartwheels. "Not a problem." I smiled. "Not a problem at all."

Eight

Two days after the Bridal Bazaar I got an email from Christine. She asked me to send her a contract for my services at her wedding, which was in three weeks.

It was official! I finally had my first real wedding job lined up. I was just weeks away from being able to call myself a bona fide wedding pianist.

I was surprised—and a little bit nervous—to hear that they weren't having a rehearsal the day before the wedding. But Christine assured me that everything was pretty straightforward and her wedding coordinator, Jamie, would tell me anything I needed to know and answer any questions I might have.

Over the next three weeks I perfected the pieces I would play for the prelude. I also learned Christine's requests: "Somewhere Over the Rainbow" for the processional, "Here Comes the Sun" for the Bridal March, and "Signed, Sealed, Delivered" for the recessional.

I debated at length over what to wear and how I should do my hair. I finally decided on a black dress with long sleeves and a mint-green scarf, and I would put my hair in a French twist—with a lot of hair spray.

Meanwhile, as I waited for the day of my first professional job, besides learning new music, I also learned how to make chicken pot pie and white bean chili. And thankfully, they were both easier than the lasagna.

* * *

The church was in the older, historical section of Madison. I arrived early so that I'd have plenty of time to find Jamie and make sure I understood all the details.

I walked up the stone steps and through one of the red wooden doors. Then I went into the sanctuary. With huge stained glass windows on either side, and a high ceiling with wooden beams and hanging lanterns, it was quite impressive.

A dark-haired guy wearing a gray jacket with a blue tie was standing near the front pew leafing through a bunch of papers. He looked college-aged.

When he heard me come in he glanced in my direction and said, "I think Uncle Kenny is still upstairs helping the groomsmen get ready."

I looked behind me. There was nobody else around. "I'm sorry, were you talking to me?" I asked as I walked to the front of the room.

He squinted and took a few steps toward me. "Oh, wait. You're not Aunt Carol," he said with a nervous laugh. "Her hair is the same color as yours."

"Oh, I'm not a guest. I'm the piano player for the ceremony."

"Oh!" He looked slightly alarmed. He began shuffling through the papers in his hand more quickly. One went flying and fluttered gently to the floor. "I'm sorry. I didn't realize you were supposed to be here already."

"I'm a little early," I explained, wondering why this person, who I guessed was a relative, would know or care when the piano player was supposed to arrive.

He reached down and snatched the wayward paper off the floor. "Okay, good." He took a pencil from behind his ear and marked something on one of the papers. "Pianist has arrived!" He looked up and laughed nervously again, then he suddenly extended his hand. "I'm sorry, I should have introduced myself. I'm Jamie, the groom's cousin."

"I'm Heather." I was feeling a little confused as I shook his hand. Jamie? Surely he wasn't …

"I'm the wedding coordinator for today." He started writing again. "Oops, my pencil just broke. Do you have one I could use?"

"Uh … yeah." I rummaged through my purse and handed him a green mechanical pencil.

He took it and scribbled on a piece of paper against his palm.

"That looks really uncomfortable," I said. "Maybe you should use something to write on?"

"Yeah!" he said. His eyes lit up. "Do you have a music book that I could use? That would be great."

"Okay." That wasn't exactly what I had in mind, but I reached into my bag again and handed him *The Essential Wedding Collection.*

"Thanks," he said, putting the papers on the book and writing some more. "I'm so nervous. I've never done this before."

I felt a knot in the pit of my stomach. "You haven't?"

"No." He finished whatever he was writing and put my pencil behind his ear. "I don't even know that much about weddings, but Christine and Matt just asked me to help them out, so I said I would."

The ramifications of what he'd just told me were sinking in. Here was the guy who was supposed to clue me in on exactly how this all worked and he knew next to nothing. Heck, I probably knew more than he did. We were in big trouble.

"Um, could I have my pencil back?" I asked.

"Oh, oh yeah, of course." He grabbed it from behind his ear and handed it to me. "Oh, and I guess you need your music too." He put out his hand with the bunch of papers. "No, wait. Heh heh." He pulled the book out from under the papers and gave it to me. "That one is yours."

"Thank you," I said, putting the book and pencil back in my bag. "So, I guess you should tell me where you'll be when you give me the cues."

"Cues?" Jamie sounded as though he had no idea what I was talking about.

The knot in my stomach got a little tighter. "I need you to cue me when the processional is about to begin, when the bride is ready to enter, that kind of thing."

"Oh, right," he said with a nod.

He continued nodding slowly. Unfortunately, I had the distinct impression that he still had no idea what I was talking about.

"I, um …" Jamie glanced around the room. "Uh, I'll get back to you about that, okay? Oh, I just remembered that I was supposed to ask the officiant something. Let me see if I can find him. Uh …" He looked around helplessly for a moment. Then, with a sudden air of authority, he announced, "There's the piano!" With a fanciful gesture he motioned toward the shiny baby grand in the front of the sanctuary as he turned and left the room.

Okay, then, I thought. I walked over to the piano, set up my music, and looked at my watch. Based on the research I'd done, I learned that the ceremony musician starts playing thirty minutes before the ceremony.

At exactly 5 o'clock I dove into my music. I started with Bach Invention 13 in A Minor. As I played the songs I'd been so carefully perfecting at home, the guests began trickling in.

By the time I started the last piece, MacDowell's "To a Wild Rose," I figured that the ceremony was probably about to begin any minute. I needed to be ready for Jamie's cue. But, come to think of it, he never did tell me where he'd be or how he was going to cue me.

I checked my watch again—5:16. What? How could it only be *5:16*?!

Is my watch wrong? I thought wildly as I continued playing. Had I really only been playing for sixteen minutes? I felt like I had tons of music prepared. It never even occurred to me to time exactly how long it took to play everything. What was I supposed to do for the next eighteen minutes?

No, wait. This wasn't really a problem. Once I finished playing "To a Wild Rose," I would just go back to the first piece and play through everything one more time. Guests were still arriving, so they wouldn't all have heard the earlier pieces. And even if some people had, well, so what? They weren't going to think: She already played Bach

Invention 13 in A Minor about ten minutes ago. What's wrong with that pianist?

There was no reason to panic. When I finished "To a Wild Rose" I went back to the top of my list and started again.

At 5:32, as I began playing Bach Invention 13 for a third time, there was still no sign of Jamie—or any member of the bridal party. Then I began to panic. If people aren't already catching on, they certainly will if I play all these pieces a fourth time, I thought.

Thankfully, Jamie appeared through a door in the back corner a few minutes later. He walked down the outer aisle toward me.

Jamie crouched down next to the piano bench. "We have a little problem," he whispered. "Just keep playing." And with that, he headed back the way he came and out the door.

A *problem*? What did that mean? What kind of problem? And how long was this *problem* going to take to get fixed?

At 6:05 I started playing Bach Invention 13 for the sixth time. It was obvious that some of the guests were getting restless. Some of them were shifting their weight and looking around, but others just seemed bored. One teenage boy was sitting with his head in his hands and his elbows on his knees, looking as though he was about to doze off. A woman about my age with her hair in a bun checked her watch, looked around the room, and then gave an exasperated sigh.

What was going on? Were we all trapped in some bizarre circle of hell, doomed to keep listening to these same pieces over and over and over?

Out of the corner of my eye, I saw a woman wearing a long teal dress enter the back of the room. She was carrying a bouquet of white roses.

What the? The processional was starting just like that? Why didn't anyone tell me?

With my heart pounding, I yanked my book off the piano and tossed it on the floor. I fumbled for what felt like forever to slap up the music to "Somewhere Over the Rainbow."

I figured out the rest of my cues by myself. Christine standing in the back of the room in her white wedding gown was a pretty good hint that I should play "Here Comes the Sun" for her entrance. And at the end of the ceremony, when the officiant announced the couple, I knew it was time to play "Signed, Sealed, Delivered" for the recessional. Well, that, plus the fact that the officiant turned and gave me a *look* when there was a long silence after her announcement.

When the recessional was over and most of the guests had filed out of the room, I was packing up my things. Jamie trudged up to me, looking exhausted and slightly pale.

"Well, we did it," he said. It sounded more like a question. "Here." He handed me an envelope with my name on it. "This is from Matt and Christine."

"Oh, right. Thanks." I'd been so concerned with everything else that I'd forgotten all about actually getting paid. "So what happened earlier? What was the problem?"

"The best man left the ring in his hotel room and had to go back and get it," said Jamie with a long sigh. "Thanks for covering."

"Sure." I slung my bag over my shoulder. "So I guess we're both experienced wedding pros now."

"Yeah." He smiled weakly. "I'm just glad it's over." In spite of how nerve-wracking the whole thing had been, I couldn't help feeling happy as I walked across the parking lot. I'd actually played the piano in public again, and I'd even been paid to do it!

And if I could do it once, then I could do it again.

Nine

That Monday afternoon I sat down at the kitchen table with a box of cards and a black pen. I hardly ever wrote actual letters or sent snail mail anymore, but I thought that sending Christine and Matt a personal thank you note—with a business card enclosed, of course—would be a nice touch.

"Mom!" Angela yelled from down the hall. "Mom!"

Nuts, the pen was out of ink. I tried scribbling on the back flap of the envelope but it didn't help. "Yes, Angela, what is it?"

"Danny keeps calling me a snoober blaster cannonball!"

I got up, tossed the pen in the garbage, and started searching around in a drawer for another one.

"Mom!" Angela shrieked. "Didn't you hear me? Danny keeps calling ... there! He just did it again!"

"Danny, don't call your sister names!" I yelled as I sat down at the table with a new pen.

Dear Christine and Matt,

"Mo-om!" Danny called.

I sighed. "What now?"

"Angela won't give me back my superhero duck!"

"I'm just looking at it for a minute!" Angela yelled. "Don't be such a baby!"

"Don't call me a baby!" Danny screamed.

"Well, don't you call me a snooper blooper ball!"

"It's a snoober blaster cannonball!" Danny yelled. "Don't you know anything?"

"I know that you're a little snoober booper butthead!" said Angela.

"Mo-om!" Danny howled. "Angela called me a bad name."

"Angela, if he's bothering you so much, just go in another room!" I yelled.

Thank you for snoober …

"Oh for heaven's sake!" I muttered as I tossed the pen down and ripped up the card.

"MOM!!!" Angela shrieked. "Mom!"

I slammed my hand down on the table. "Enough! I am trying to concentrate! Just find something to do and leave each other alone!"

I took another card out of the box. As I was about to start writing I heard footsteps pounding toward me.

"But Mommy!" Angela squealed as she ran into the kitchen. "It's an emergency! Danny has a Barbie shoe stuck up his nose!"

I turned around. "He what?"

"He has a Barbie shoe stuck up his nose!" She pointed down the hallway in a panic. "Come quick!"

I blinked. "How did a … ? Oh, never mind." I jumped up and followed her down the hall.

Danny was on the floor of Angela's room. He was breathing loudly through his mouth and poking his finger up his right nostril.

"No!" Angela said. "Don't poke it. You'll just shove it further up!"

Danny pulled his finger out of his nose. "Really? Do you think it could go all the way up into my brain? That'd be cool!"

"Mommy!" Angela wailed.

"Everybody calm down," I said, kneeling on the floor next to Danny. "I've never heard of people getting Barbie footwear lodged in their brains, and I doubt you'll be the first. Come here Danny." I gently pulled Danny's hands away from his face and tilted his chin up. Sure enough, there was a tiny pink bump about halfway up his nostril.

Angela looked at me anxiously. "How are you going to get it out?"

That was, in fact, an excellent question. I thought about it for a moment.

"Well …" I said.

Both kids were staring at me.

"I think, I think that the best way to get it out … would be …"

The kids leaned in a little closer.

Rats. I was kind of hoping that *they* would come up with something.

"Um … okay, let's try something," I said. "Danny, take a deep breath in through your mouth, and then blow it out as hard as you can through your nose."

Danny nodded, sucked up a loud gulp of air, then made a noise through his mouth that sounded like *Fffff … aaahhh*!!

"No, no." I pressed my hand against my forehead and shook my head. "You're supposed to be blowing out through your nose, not your mouth. The whole idea is that the air goes through your nose and pushes out the shoe. Got it?"

Danny nodded, but he didn't look so sure.

"Okay, are you ready to try again?" I asked.

He nodded. Then he took a big breath through his mouth and made a pitiful little sniffle through his nose.

I waited.

Danny stared at me.

"Uh … was that it?" I asked.

"Uh-huh. Did it come out?" Danny eagerly looked around the room.

"No." I rested my head in my hands. "No, it didn't." I took a deep breath and tried to refocus. "Here, let's try this. Press your left nostril shut with your finger. No. Your left one … no, see the one I'm pointing at? The one without the shoe in it. That's it! Okay, now hold it shut, and then blow as hard as you can out your nose, okay?"

Danny nodded. He pressed against the side of his nose and made a faint sniff.

I ran my hand through my hair. Blowing it out was probably not going to work.

"Okay, don't worry," I said. "We'll just try something else."

I had no idea what that something else would be, but surely my child wasn't the first to get a small object lodged in his nostril. I'd never heard of a twenty-two-year-old who'd been walking around for over a decade with a toy permanently stuck up his nose. There had to be some way to get it out.

Angela jumped up. "I know!" she said, running out of the room.

I ruffled Danny's hair while I wondered what Angela would come back with. A flashlight? A magnifying glass? Something ridiculous, like a hammer?

Danny looked up at me, his eyes huge and terrified. "Is she gonna hurt me?"

"I don't think so," I assured him, although I wasn't completely sure myself.

"Here Danny!" Angela said, running back into the room with the pepper shaker. "Pepper makes people sneeze." She unscrewed the top. "So take a few good whiffs and you can sneeze it out."

Huh. That might actually work.

Danny obediently leaned forward and took a few sniffs. He wrinkled his nose a few times, but other than that, nothing happened.

"You're not getting close enough," Angela said, practically shoving the pepper up his nose.

Danny sniffed again. Nothing.

"Maybe we need to put some pepper in his nose," said Angela.

"I don't think so," I said.

"Why not?" Angela asked.

"Call it a hunch," I said, eying Danny carefully. "Somehow, shoving even more things up his nose just doesn't sound like the best plan right now."

"Come on Danny!" Angela yelled, ramming the pepper shaker against his nose. "Breathe in the pepper!"

"Ow!" Danny screeched.

"Angela," I said, "you can't force him to …"

"Ah … achoo!" Danny sneezed.

Angela and I leaned forward. We were staring intently to see if a shoe would come flying out of Danny's nose. Unfortunately, we had no such luck.

I tilted Danny's head and looked up his nose. "No change," I reported. "It's really stuck up there. I don't think sneezing is going to do it."

"So what are we going to do?" Angela asked.

I sighed. "I think we might have to go to the pediatrician."

I'd been dreading this but didn't see any way around it. I looked at my watch. It was almost ten minutes after 5. Of course it was. My children didn't have the courtesy to shove small objects into their body cavities during office hours.

"Scratch that," I said. "The doctor's office just closed for the day. We may have to go to the emergency room."

Danny scrambled to his feet. "The emergency room? Does that mean we get to ride in an ambulance?"

I shook my head. "No. I'll drive us."

"Oh." His face fell for a second, then lit up again. "Will I need an operation? Are they gonna drill a hole through my nose?"

Angela made a face. "Eww!"

"Will I have my own hospital room?" Danny asked. "And will I get to ride up and down the hall in a wheelchair?"

"I don't think it's going to be anything that exciting," I said. "Here, let me call your dad and tell him what's going on. You guys go get your shoes and coats on. Oh, and both of you go to the bathroom."

The kids scurried out of the room and I went to the living room. I dialed Steve's work number.

"Hello."

"Hi, it's me," I said. "Danny has a Barbie shoe stuck up his nose and it's jammed up there too far for me to get it out. We tried to get him to sneeze it out, but that didn't work, even when we used pepper. So I was thinking of taking him to the emergency room. Does that sound like a good plan to you?"

There was silence on the other end.

"He has a what stuck up where?" Steve asked.

"A Barbie shoe, up his nose."

Silence again.

"How?" Steve asked.

"I don't know. I wasn't in the room at the time." I glanced down the hall toward the kids' rooms. "I think I'm afraid to ask."

Steve gave a long sigh. "Yeah, sure, take him to the ER. Do you want me to try to get off work a little early so I can meet you guys there?"

"Thanks, but no. I think we can manage. The ER is way on the other side of town from your office anyway."

"Okay … well, good luck," said Steve.

"Thanks. Bye."

I hung up and called down the hall, "Are you kids ready to go?"

Danny appeared with an arm in one coat sleeve and the other sleeve dragging on the floor. He was wearing a sneaker on one foot and the other foot only had a red sock.

"I can't find my other sneaker," he said.

I took a deep breath and tried not to lose my temper. "What do you mean, you can't find it?"

He looked slightly puzzled. "I mean … I went in my closet and I only saw one sneaker, and I don't know where the other one is."

"Oh for heaven's sake," I said, heading past him toward his closet. "Hey, Angela, are you ready to go?"

"Almost," she called from her bedroom. "I just want to change clothes first."

"Change clothes?" I rolled my eyes. "You don't happen to know where Danny's other sneaker is, do you?" I realized that this was probably a pointless question.

"It should be in his closet," she informed me.

"Yes, you'd think so," I muttered, crawling around on the closet floor, shoving aside a Lightning McQueen baseball cap, two candy wrappers, a green stuffed frog that I forgot he even had, several scattered Matchbox cars, and a library copy of *Katy and the Big Snow*. But there was no sign of any sneaker.

"Danny," I said, sitting back on my heels, "let's not waste time worrying about this. Why don't you just wear your dress shoes?"

"They don't fit me anymore."

I took a deep breath and slowly let it out. "What do you mean, they don't fit you? Since when?"

"I don't know. Since the day I tried to put them on and they didn't fit."

"Okay, I'm ready," Angela announced, walking into the room wearing the princess costume she'd worn for Halloween.

"What are you doing?" I asked.

Angela looked hurt. "I wanted to wear something special. Don't you think I look pretty?"

"Yes. Yes, you look very pretty," I told her. "But I'm not sure that …"

Hey eyes pleaded at me from behind her glasses.

"Okay, fine." I flipped my hand in the air. "Wear that if you want to."

Angela smiled. In fact, she was beaming.

I turned back to the closet, scooped the stray candy wrappers off the floor, and threw them in the trash basket. "Danny, just try the dress shoes on anyway. Maybe you just imagined that they were too tight, or maybe you were … I don't know … wearing really thick socks that day or something." I passed him the shoes with one hand while trying to gather up the Matchbox cars with the other.

"Are we leaving yet?" Angela asked.

"We have to finish getting your brother dressed first."

Danny put his unshod foot into the loafer. "Mom, it doesn't fit!" he insisted. "It hurts! It's too tight!"

I tried to push his heel into the shoe.

"Ow!" he yelled.

He was right. They didn't fit anymore, at all.

"This is ridiculous," I muttered, tugging the shoe off his foot. "You've probably only worn these shoes three times since we bought them."

"I told you," he said.

"Are we leaving yet?" Angela asked again.

I threw the shoes into the hallway. "We'll put those in a charity bag later. Are those the only two pairs of shoes you have?"

"Uh-huh," said Danny.

"Well, we can't have you walking through the hospital parking lot with no shoes on." I thought for a moment, then I tossed him the bear claw slippers that Steve's mother had given both kids last Christmas. "Here, you'll just have to wear your slippers today."

"Oh, wow!" Angela said. "If he gets to wear his bear slippers I wanna wear mine too." She ran out of the room.

Danny slid the bear claws onto his feet, oblivious to the fact that half his coat was still dangling off him.

"Here," I said, "let me help you finish getting your coat on."

"Don't forget Bunny-Bun!" Angela cried as she ran back into the room. She'd accessorized her pink princess costume with her bear claw slippers.

"Um," I said, "that's an interesting combination."

She glanced down at her outfit, then back up at me with a worried look. "You're right," she said. "Let me go change clothes again." She turned around and headed toward her room.

"No! Wait!" I yelled. "Please! That's not what I meant! We don't have time to …"

The slam of her bedroom door cut me off. I turned to Danny who was finally dressed, albeit with bear claw slippers on his feet.

"We can't leave without Bunny-Bun," he said, "and I don't know where he is."

I buried my face in my hands and took a deep breath. It's a good thing that the emergency room never closes, I thought.

* * *

We walked into the emergency room, both kids with bear claw slippers on their feet. I signed in and we sat down in the waiting room.

"How are you doing, Danny?" I asked as I started filling out the forms. "Does it hurt at all?"

Danny was clutching Bunny-Bun, who, it turned out, had been sitting next to the bathroom sink. He scrunched up his face, sat very still, and pondered the sensations in his nose—or lack thereof—for a moment. "It doesn't really hurt. It just feels sort of …" he sniffed a few times, "clogged up."

I nodded. "Well, I guess that's why God gave us two nostrils … just in case one of them accidentally gets plugged up with a piece of your sibling's toy." I continued filling in our address and phone number on a form.

"Can we stop at the store and buy me a new Barbie on the way home?" Angela asked. "I want a bathing beauty Barbie."

"A new Barbie?" I asked. "Why?"

"Why?" Angela yelled. "Because my Barbie's ruined. I can't have her just walking around with one shoe forever."

"I'm pretty sure we'll get the shoe out," I said, scribbling down Stephanie's name and phone number as an emergency contact.

"Eww!" Angela said. "It'll be gross. It'll have boogers and snot all over it."

"Hey!" said Danny. "My nose is not full of boogers and snot!"

"Everybody's nose is full of boogers and snot!" Angela said, her voice getting louder. "That's what a nose is for!"

A mother holding a sleepy toddler girl on her lap was sitting three chairs away from us. She looked in our direction.

I chuckled and faintly smiled at her. She didn't smile back.

"Listen," I hissed at the kids, "let's not scream about boogers in public places, okay?"

"She started it," Danny said, sticking his finger in Angela's face.

She smacked his finger aside. "Get your finger out of my face. And stop sticking my things up your nose."

"I only stuck one thing up my nose," Danny retorted.

The mother of the sleepy girl continued staring at us. I chuckled again and gave her a little wave.

I set the pen down on the clipboard. "Danny, just out of curiosity, exactly why did you stick a Barbie shoe up your nose in the first place?"

He looked at me, surprised. "I wanted to see how far it would fit." He said it as if it should have been obvious.

"Uh-huh." I rolled my eyes and went to turn in all the paperwork.

About ten minutes later a nurse called for us. I followed her down the hall to the examination room, the kids shuffling behind me in their bear claw feet.

The nurse took Danny's temperature and checked his blood pressure. "The doctor will be with you shortly," she said, sticking the chart in the door and heading out.

Twenty-five minutes later we were still waiting for the doctor, the kids' eyes glued to the cartoons on the TV. The word shortly seemed to have a different meaning to people in the medical field. Although, to be fair, they probably figured a kid with a toy jammed up his nose could wait while they tended to the kids who were, say, bleeding profusely or knocked unconscious.

The door finally opened. A short man with dark hair walked in holding a chart. "Hi there, I'm Dr. Ballon." He shook my hand without looking up from the chart. "I see we have a foreign object in the nose, is that correct?"

"Yup." Danny leaned his head back and pushed the end of his nose up with his thumb.

"I see …" Dr. Ballon studied the inside of Danny's nose for a moment. He walked over to the counter and pulled something that looked like tweezers out of a glass canister. He inserted the tweezers in Danny's nose, pulled out the pink shoe, wrapped it in a tissue, and handed it to me. "There you go."

I stared at the wad of tissue in my hand. The entire procedure had taken less than six seconds.

"You're done," Dr. Ballon said, scribbling something on the chart. "They'll be here in a minute to check you out. Have a good evening." He put the chart back in the door and shut it behind him with a click.

The three of us sat in silence for a moment.

"Is that it?" Danny asked. He sounded disappointed.

"Apparently so," I said, tucking the wrapped shoe into my purse. I'll soak it in alcohol to de-booger it when we get home, I thought.

Danny sighed.

The door opened again. A heavyset woman with her hair in a tight bun backed into the room pulling a computer table on wheels. "Okay Mrs. Hershey, we're going to check you out." She hit a bunch of keys, then said, "You have a copay of two hundred fifty dollars."

"What!" I yelped. "Two hundred fifty dollars!"

"That's correct," she said calmly, still looking at the screen. "Will that be cash or charge?"

"That's crazy!" I yelled. "The doctor was in the room for less than thirty seconds. He didn't even need a medical degree to do what he did! I could have done that myself if I'd thought of it."

Ms. Tight Bun was unmoved by my outburst.

"Your copay for today is two hundred fifty dollars," she repeated.

"That can't be right," I said, hunting around in my purse. I opened my wallet, yanked out my insurance card, and squinted at the fine print on the bottom. "Aha! There!" I yelled, sticking the card in her face. "It says right there that the urgent care copay is seventy-five dollars! Ha!"

She glanced at the card. "That's the in-network copay. We're outside your network."

"What?" I pulled the card back and squinted at it again, not even sure what I was looking for. "Since when? We were here two years ago for my daughter, and it cost ... something like ... well, I don't know, but it wasn't anywhere near two hundred fifty dollars."

She narrowed her eyes at me. "Well, has your insurance changed?"

I opened my mouth, then snapped it shut. I remembered that Steve's insurance had changed over the summer. So not only did our monthly premiums go up, but now we had crappier coverage, higher copays, and fewer options.

"I can't believe this," I muttered, handing my credit card to Ms. Tight Bun. I signed the computerized receipt, mumbled a thank you, and took each child by the hand to lead them out.

"Stupid insurance companies," I said under my breath as I snapped the car into reverse and backed out of the parking spot. "Who's running this country anyway? I bet nobody in France has to pay two hundred fifty dollars to have a doctor slide tweezers into their kid's nose."

The more I thought about it, the angrier and more stressed out I got. I drove all the way home with my jaw clenched and my hands tightly gripping the steering wheel. I vaguely recall overhearing Danny explaining the difference between Marvel and DC Comics to Angela in the back seat.

When we got home I walked through the front door and took approximately six steps before tripping over a pile of about thirty plastic zoo animals. "Who left all this here?!" I yelled, picking up a plastic giraffe and tossing it onto the couch. "And look at this whole room! It's a mess! It's always a mess!" I sank into a chair, no longer feeling angry, but simply exhausted. "No wonder we couldn't find your shoe."

Steve appeared in the kitchen doorway, munching a bowl of cereal. "Hey, you're back. Did they get the thing out of Danny's nose?"

"Oh yes," I said. "It took about six seconds and cost us two hundred fifty dollars!"

Steve's eyes got big. "Ouch."

"And look at this place! Toys everywhere, shoes that don't even fit, a whole bunch of crap we don't need cluttering up everything so much that I can't even think straight."

Steve ate another spoonful of cereal. "So get rid of it," he said with his mouth full.

"Get rid of it?"

He shrugged. "If you don't need it and it's bugging you, then get rid of some of it."

"Of course," I said slowly. I jumped out of the chair and threw my arms around him, practically knocking the cereal bowl out of his hands. "Of course! You're a genius!"

"Really? Saying *that* makes me a genius?"

"It's not that!" I said, turning quickly toward the kids who both looked completely confused. I turned back to Steve. "Don't you see?"

All three heads slowly shook back and forth in silence.

"We'll have a garage sale!" I announced, throwing my hands triumphantly in the air. "Then we'll not only get rid of all this junk …"

"Our stuff's not junk!" Danny protested.

"But," I said, "if we sell some of it we'll get enough money to pay the hospital bill, and maybe even the traffic ticket, and … and …"

Steve looked doubtful. "You really think our junk is worth over two hundred bucks?"

"It's not junk!" Danny insisted.

"Sure," I said. "I mean, it's not just the kids' stuff. I've got a bunch of stuff in my closet that I never wear anymore, and all those shelves in the computer room could probably do with some thinning out."

"Hey!" said Steve. "Don't touch those shelves. That's where I keep my old comic books and all my Star Wars collectibles."

"Okay, fine," I said with a grin. "The comic books and Star Wars collectibles can stay. But the garage sale is on!"

Ten

"This Hello Kitty puzzle is missing a piece," announced a woman with a baggy blue T-shirt and straight brown hair almost down to her waist. She dropped the box on the table with a bang. "I counted them."

"Oh, I'm sorry," I said. "Are you sure? I thought I checked all the …"

"Of course I'm sure," she interrupted. "I counted them and there's only ninety-nine pieces. I know how to count."

"Oh … kay," I said. "Well, if it's missing a piece, you're welcome to just have it for free. We're done with …"

"I don't want a puzzle with a missing piece. I just thought you should know." She glared at me, then turned and headed for the table of children's books.

Perhaps she's on a quest to inspect *Goodnight Moon* and *Hippos Go Berserk*! for any imperfections, I thought.

Steve came outside and walked over to my sale table on the edge of the driveway. He was holding a cup of coffee in one hand and a folding chair in the other. "How's it

---

going?" He unfolded the chair and sat down next to me. "Did we make enough to offset the urgent care bill yet?"

"Not quite," I said, tipping back the mug I was using for proceeds to show him it was empty.

"Well, you've only been out here for, what, less than an hour?" Steve looked at his watch. "Maybe things will pick up."

"Maybe," I said, scrunching up my nose, "but I always thought the hardcore garage sale shoppers came super early, so I'm not sure if the crowds will pick up or fizzle out. Hey, what are the kids up to?"

As if on cue, Danny and Angela came barreling outside. They were both barefoot.

"Hi Mommy!" Danny yelled from across the driveway. His mouth was full, he was carrying a half-eaten strawberry Pop-Tart, and his red shirt was inside out.

"Can we help?" Angela asked. Her curly hair was a tangled mess, sticking straight out in some places. And her pink blouse was so wrinkled that it looked like it'd been balled up and stuffed inside a shoebox for a month.

"I'm not sure there's much to do." I was watching a man walking around our driveway, but he headed back to his car without touching anything or even slowing down. "We haven't really been getting a lot of action yet."

"Oh." Angela sounded disappointed. She looked around and frowned for a moment. Then her eyes lit up. "I know what to do! Hang on, I'll be right back!" She disappeared into the house, unkempt hair flying behind her.

Steve and I exchanged looks.

"Any idea what she's doing?" Steve asked. "You know them better than I do."

"You got me," I said. "I never know what's going on around here either. But we could use all the help we can get."

A car slowed down as it was driving by. It paused in front of our house for a few seconds before speeding off down the street.

Danny climbed into my lap. He was still eating his Pop-Tart.

A woman with a blond ponytail pushing a toddler in an umbrella stroller walked up to the table. She set down a pile of clothes. "I'll take these."

"Great." I gave Steve a quick smile and started sorting through the clothes. "Let's see, this blouse is four dollars, and another four for the jeans makes eight, this dress is seven dollars ..."

"Hey!" Danny said excitedly as he hopped off my lap. "She's buying that dress that you hate!"

"Oh ... heh heh." I covered up the dress with the jeans. "That's the beauty of a garage sale, Danny. We can get rid of what we don't want anymore, and other people can enjoy ..."

"But you said no one would ever buy that dress!" Danny was obviously thrilled at our triumph. "I heard you tell Dad that the fabric was cheap and that it made you look like an eggplant and the only reason you even kept it that long was because it was a gift from Grandma."

The woman with the ponytail lifted the dress out from under the jeans. She held it up and frowned.

"There's nothing wrong with the dress," Steve said to Danny. "It just isn't a good color for your mom. It would probably look better on a blond."

The woman either didn't hear Steve, or she simply wasn't interested in his fashion opinions. She turned the dress from back to front, rubbed the fabric between her thumb and forefinger, and folded it back up.

"I think I'll pass on this after all," she said, setting the dress off to the side and looking through the rest of the clothes in her pile. "And I don't think I'll get this one … or this one … and I guess I don't really need this one either." She pushed the four items in her discard pile toward me and patted the two remaining toddler shirts. "Just these."

"Great," I said, forcing myself to smile. "That'll be six dollars."

The woman gave me the money and thanked me. She put the two shirts in her stroller basket and headed off happily.

Steve and I looked at each other. Then we both slowly turned to glare at Danny.

"What?" he asked innocently. "What did I do?"

"We don't need any commentary on the merchandise," Steve said quietly.

Danny contorted his face. "What's that mean?"

"It means," I sighed, "that you just cost us almost thirty dollars." I tilted the mug toward me. "Although, at least this isn't empty anymore."

"Maaahh-MEEEEEE!!" Angela shrieked from inside the house.

The three of us, well, probably everybody at the garage sale, whipped around.

Angela came running out of the garage, her arms flailing. "Come quick!"

"What is it?" I asked.

"I was making …" she was speaking between gasps and sobs, " … lemonade so we could sell it to everybody … who comes. I … I filled the pitcher with water and lemon juice … and then when I reached for the sugar canister I … knocked the pitcher over and … the whole thing spilled on the floor. I … I tried to grab it when it spilled and … I knocked the sugar off the counter and the canister broke … and there's sugar all over the kitchen floor … and when I tried to clean it up I cut my thumb … on one of the broken pieces … and now it's bleeding. So I … I started to run and get you but the kitchen floor was … all wet so I slipped and fell … and now my bottom hurts!" She made a snuffling sound, ran the back of her hand against her nose, and gulped for breath.

My brain hadn't comprehended all of that, nor was it sure that it even wanted to. But I was pretty sure I heard the word bleeding somewhere in there. "Let me see."

She held out her thumb. There was a round blob of blood on it.

"Oh, it'll be fine," I said. "We just need to wash it and put a Band-Aid on it."

"I didn't know you knew how to make lemonade," Steve said to Angela.

She gave him a surprised look. "Mommy taught us how to cook, remember?" she said, jabbing her bloodied thumb in my direction. "I can make anything now."

"Ah, of course." Steve gave me an amused smile.

I sighed. I guess we all eventually rue the day we teach our kids to be self-reliant, I thought.

"Here," Steve said wearily, pushing against the table as he stood up. "I'll deal with this one Heather. You just stay and be ready for the flood of customers when they come."

"Oh, thank you!" I gushed, not even wanting to imagine the sticky wet mess that was waiting in the kitchen, or the army of ants preparing to charge in from all ends of the Earth. "Thank you thank you thank you thank you thank you thank you thank you."

"Should I go help too?" Danny asked, leaping up as Steve and Angela started toward the house.

"No!" Steve yelled. "Uh, I mean …"

"You stay here and keep me company, Danny." I patted the chair that Steve had been sitting in. "Just don't comment on what people buy, okay?"

"Okay." Danny plopped down in the chair just as a man with a baseball cap approached the table.

The man began lining up several of Danny's Fisher-Price vehicles. "I'll take these."

Hurray! Not only was he buying five items, but they were all close to ten dollars each. "Okay, great. Let's see, that's a total of …"

"NOOO!!!" Danny bellowed, jumping up. "Those are mine!"

The man raised his eyebrows at me.

"Oh … heh heh." I laughed. "He hasn't played with these since preschool. He's just being silly, aren't you, Danny?" I playfully ruffled his hair.

Danny was not amused. He jerked away from me. "These are mine!" He snatched the fire engine with one hand and the tow truck with the other. "He can't have them!"

Two shoppers who were digging through piles of baby clothes looked up to see what all the commotion was about.

"Danny," I hissed, leaning toward him, "we talked about this yesterday. You never play with them anymore and you agreed that we could sell them. Remember? Besides, you still have a ton of other cars and trucks and trains and …"

"I never said that!" Danny screeched. He frantically scooped up all five toys and hugged them against his chest. "I love these! They're my favorites! I never said you could sell them!"

"That's not true, of course," I said to the man. "We really did talk about this yesterday, and he really did insist that we …"

"Hey, look," said the man, "I don't want to take them away from him if he loves them that much."

"No!" I said desperately. "No, he really doesn't love them that much! Trust me, they've been sitting on the floor of the playroom untouched for four months, at least! And he spends most of his time these days playing with his Matchbox cars and Hot Wheels, and … and he has way too many toys anyway! I mean, they're just piled up everywhere and last week we couldn't even find his sneakers after he stuck his sister's Barbie shoe up his nose, and we all had to run to the emergency room with him wearing his bear claw slippers that his grandma gave him, and …"

The man held up his hand. "It's okay. I don't mind one bit. You can keep them, buddy," he said to Danny. "Hey, gimme five."

Danny looked surprised. He grinned and whacked the man's hand as hard as he could.

"Have a great day," said the man. He winked at Danny before he strode off.

AARRRGH!!!

I let my forehead drop down to the table.

"Isn't it great Mommy?" said Danny. "I get to keep them after all."

"Yeah, great," I mumbled into the table before slowing raising my head. "Danny, do you know what the purpose of a garage sale is?"

He cocked his head to one side and stared at me.

"The purpose of a garage sale is to sell things and make money. We *want* people to buy these things. That's the reason we spent half the week gathering and tagging all this stuff, and why I'm spending half of my weekend sitting here watching total strangers poking through our things."

He continued to stare at me, confused.

I sighed. "Never mind. I get it. You love your trucks. Well, if we're not going to sell them, why don't you go ahead and put them back inside. Oh, and ask your dad and Angela if they need me to do anything."

I watched Danny scamper toward the house using his inside out shirt like a pouch to carry the toys. When I turned back around a girl who looked about eleven was standing at the table.

"Can I help you?" I asked, wondering how long she'd been standing there.

She nodded slowly. "I … have a question about the board games over there."

"Okay."

She didn't reply.

I tilted my head. "So, what's your question?"

She glanced over her shoulder, then back at me. "What?"

Apparently, kids aren't any less weird as they grow older, I thought.

"I'm sorry," I said. "Did you say that you had a question for me?"

"Oh yeah, right." She looked uncomfortable. "Yeah, I need you to come over there. I need to show you something."

"Okay, sure." I shrugged, stood up, and followed her to the table with the board games. "What did you want to know?"

"Um, yeah ..." Her eyes darted around a few times, then she slowly picked Candy Land off the top of the stack. "Is this for sale?"

"Is it for *sale*?" I repeated.

"Yeah, well, like, I know it's for sale, but ... is it any good?"

"Well, it's a good game for preschoolers. Are you planning to buy it for a younger sibling?"

"Uh ... yeah, sure," she said, shrugging. "Like, how do you play it?"

"Well, you take turns picking cards that tell you what color to move to on the path. The first player who reaches the ..."

"Never mind." The girl tossed the box back onto the table and started walking away. "Thanks."

I shook my head and put the game back on top of the stack, straightening the box so that it lined up with the Hi-Ho! Cherry-O game underneath.

Out of the corner of my eye, I saw the girl with a man. Was that her father? They were near the end of my driveway, hurrying toward the street. Okay, now this was really weird. It was almost like they were ...

Wait a minute. Was it possible? I darted back to the sale table and picked up my mug. It was empty. *Completely empty*!

"Hey! HEY!!" I screamed as I ran toward the edge of the driveway.

They walked faster, jumped in a car, and slammed the doors.

"YOU THIEF!" I yelled, running down my driveway as they sped away. "Come back here! Yeah, you!" I was shaking my fist in the air even though I knew it was a lost cause at that point. "You despicable person, getting your own child to help you steal! And for what? Fourteen measly dollars? You lousy garage sale shoppers are all so cheap!"

I turned around. Five garage sale shoppers were all staring at me. "Well," I said, "not you, of course. I meant that guy!" I jabbed my finger in the direction of the street.

I was met with an uncomfortable silence and some shifty eyes. I'm sure people were wondering if the woman with all the junk piled in her driveway was mentally unbalanced.

"Uh, anyway …" I coughed and walked calmly back to my chair, forcing a smile. "Enjoy your shopping everybody! Just let me know if you need anything."

I got a couple dubious looks before everyone went back to rooting through our stuff.

Steve came outside. Both kids were trailing behind him. "Okay, I think we got the kitchen under control. I added sugar to your grocery list, and Mr. Clean. Oh, and you might want to buy a new sugar container. I just put it in a Tupperware one for now."

"I got a pink Band-Aid!" Angela announced, showing me her thumb.

"You guys missed the excitement," I said. "Someone stole all our proceeds, or profits, or net, uh … Well, anyway, someone stole all the money while you were inside."

"What?" Steve asked. "What happened?"

"I was tricked by an eleven-year-old," I muttered.

"How much did they take?"

"All of it. Fourteen dollars."

"Oh." Steve considered for a moment, then shrugged. "Well, then maybe we should be glad the sale has been a big failure so far."

I was about to say something when someone said, "Excuse me."

A man was holding a little boy's hand. The boy was a bit younger than Danny, bouncing up and down on the man's feet.

"Could we go inside and use your bathroom?" the man asked. "My son really has to go."

I knew that bounce all too well. "Oh, sure," I said, gesturing toward the house. "If you go right in through the garage and then ..." I saw Steve raising his eyebrows at me. "Uh ... then into the, um ..."

"We're having some plumbing issues today," Steve said firmly. "The bathrooms aren't working."

"Uh ... right," I said. "We're waiting for the plumber to come. He should be here any minute, actually." I looked up and down the street as if I was watching for a truck. "And I sure hope he comes soon because it's really difficult having kids and, uh ... no bathroom." I cleared my throat and avoided the man's eyes.

Steve looked at me like I was crazy.

The man sighed and his son started bouncing faster. "Are you sure? We'll just be a minute. He really has to go."

"Sorry," said Steve. He pointed down the street. "If you go down to the end of the street, turn left, and then turn left again onto McMurray Road, there's a group of fast-food restaurants not too far."

"Right," I added quickly. "That's where we've been going."

Steve gave me that strange look again.

The man looked at us steadily for a moment. I tried to look everywhere but at him.

"All right," he finally said. "Thank you."

His son tugged his hand as they walked away. "Come on, Dad!"

After a few seconds I whispered to Steve. "I felt bad lying to them."

"You did?" Steve asked. "It sounded to me like you were having fun with it."

"Well, I had to make it believable. And I still think we should've let them use the bathroom. That poor kid."

"What are you, crazy?" Steve whispered. "You just told me somebody ran off with all the money you made. Now you want total strangers wandering around inside our house?"

"Well, you could've gone with them and waited in the hallway. What did you think would happen?"

"I have no idea, and I didn't want to find out. Don't worry, they'll be fine."

A blue rubber ball the kids had been kicking around in the front yard came bouncing past us. Angela was running after it.

She picked up the ball. "Hey," she said, pointing behind her. "What's for sale back there?"

"Where?" I leaned over the table and turned my head. I couldn't see anything.

"In the backyard by the bushes," said Angela. "There's a boy and his dad back there."

Wait a minute. There was a boy and his dad in our backyard by the bushes? Surely they weren't … They couldn't actually be … I jumped out of my chair and ran around to the front of the table where Angela was. They *were*.

I clapped my hand to my mouth. "Steeeeve!"

"What?" he said, walking around the table to see what we were looking at. "Oh, well, that's one solution."

"Don't look!" I squealed and swatted the air with my hand. "Everybody turn around!"

None of us moved.

"Angela, gimme the ball!" Danny yelled as he ran up to us. He stopped and followed our stares. "Hey, that boy's peeing in our yard!"

"Shush!" I said, looking down at the pavement and shielding my eyes with my hand. "Okay, everybody quit staring! Turn around!" I slightly turned each kid's shoulders before going back to my chair, folding my hands on the table, and looking straight ahead.

Danny looked toward the backyard and started laughing.

"Don't look!" I said. "And don't laugh! Are they done yet? Aaahh! No, forget I said that! Turn around! Quit looking!" I looked at the street and put my hand up to the side of my face. "Eww eww eww … what kind of people do something like that?"

"I guess he really had to go." Steve walked back to his chair and sat down next to me.

I turned around to face him. "This is all your fault! If you'd just let that poor child use our bathroom when they asked us, this never would have happened."

Steve shrugged. "Eh, it's not that big a deal."

"Not that big a deal? A stranger is peeing in our backyard!"

"Well, we weren't exactly in danger of winning Yard of the Month to begin with. A new brown spot won't make that much difference."

I shuddered.

"Here they come," said Danny. He was still staring right at them, despite everything I'd said.

I waved my arms frantically. "Okay, everybody pretend we didn't see anything. Kids, turn around and face me and daddy. Here, everybody pretend we're in the middle of some fascinating conversation like we never noticed anything."

Steve leaned across the table. "Kids," he said gravely, "it's time to finally tell you the truth. Your mother and I aren't really who we say we are. While you're asleep at night, we put on our superhero outfits and fight crime."

Danny's eyes got huge. "Really?"

"Oh, for heaven's sake!" I said. "He's joking. Steve, cut it out."

"What?" Steve asked innocently. "You told us to have a fascinating conversation."

The father and son who'd just been using our backyard as a toilet walked past us down the driveway without giving us a glance. They both looked quite happy with themselves.

There was dead silence for about four seconds. Then, Steve and the kids all burst out laughing.

"Hush!" I whispered. "They could still hear you!"

"This is fun!" Danny said, still laughing. "We should have a garage sale every week."

"Yes," I said, rolling my eyes. "Because this one has been so incredibly successful."

Eleven

Eighteen dollars and twelve cents was the grand total from our garage sale. Three days of digging through closets and drawers, sorting and tagging things, hauling everything out to the driveway, and spending half my Saturday sitting outside, and all I had to show for it was eighteen dollars and twelve cents.

"Heather," Steve said to me the next day, "what if … now, don't get mad at me … but what if you got some sort of part-time job? Just something temporary that brings in a little side money. You know, just until your wedding business starts picking up."

I'd been thinking the exact same thing, but I was afraid to say it. "I *really* don't want to go back to an office. I hate the work. I hate the traffic. Plus, I want to be home when the kids get home from school."

"Yeah, I want that too. So, let's see …" Steve stared off to the side, thinking, "what's something close to home that's always hiring and you'd get home around the same time as the kids?"

Our eyes met.

"Are you thinking what I'm thinking?" Steve asked.

"Unfortunately, yes," I grumbled.

* * *

I'd been hoping to substitute teach in Danny and Angela's school. But I was told at my substitute teaching orientation that the elementary school jobs were the most requested. People who were willing to work at middle schools were likely to get called more quickly and more often, especially since the school year was well under way and lot of the elementary substitute teachers were already established.

Since I was eager to get started—mostly because I was afraid that I'd change my mind and back out if I thought about it for too long—I marked the middle school box on my application. Within three days I received my first call. It was for a seventh grade math teacher.

I pulled nervously into the visitor section of the parking lot at Baker Middle School—just like I'd been advised to do during orientation. I went inside and made my way to the office.

"You'll need to sign in here, then wear this name tag all day, for security purposes," said the school secretary. "Do you know where Mrs. Thompson's room is?"

"No," I said, scribbling *Mrs. Hershey* on the name tag sticker. I peeled off the back and stuck it on my blouse. "I've never been here before."

"All right." She slapped a xeroxed copy of a map on the counter and started drawing on it. "You turn left out of the office, turn right at the second hallway, go up the flight of stairs, then take your first right. It's the second classroom on the left."

"Thank you." I took the map and walked out of the office into the sea of kids. I was trying not to get run down by the preteen boys plowing past me, oblivious to anything in their paths.

I arrived at the classroom, switched on the lights, and was greeted by a teacher's desk completely covered in mounds of paper. I dropped my purse onto the chair. I needed to find something, anything, that would enlighten me vis-à-vis what I was supposed to do when the twelve-year-olds all came barreling into the room in about ten minutes.

I started digging through the mass of scattered papers. Let's see what I find, I thought. I discovered: school announcements, this week's school lunch menu, a messy lump of what looked like graded homework assignments, and a letter from the principal about schedule changes due to Thursday's assembly. I moved the mounds around, starting to get frantic. I unearthed: two unopened envelopes addressed to Ms. Sharon Thompson, a letter from a parent, countless yellow sticky notes, a crumpled up Target receipt, a nickel, a calculator, five paper clips, and a stack of unsigned permission slips.

I finally found piece of yellow lined paper that had *Substitute Plans* and the date scribbled across the top in black ink. Aha, here we go, I thought. As I squinted at the paper trying to read Mrs. Thompson's cursive writing, two boys appeared in the doorway.

"A sub!" one announced. He was standing in the doorway staring at me.

The other boy walked across the room. He plopped into his seat and casually let his books fall onto his desk with a thud.

I smiled at them and looked back down at the yellow paper. I was able to decipher some words. *First, second, and fourth periods, give them worksheet 12A.*

"Get out of the way, Joe!" a girl yelled. "You're blocking the door!"

Joe took a step to the side. "We have a sub!" he informed his classmates as they poured into the room.

"Well, duh," said the girl as she glided past him and flounced to her seat. "I'm not blind. I can see that lady isn't Mrs. Thompson."

I smiled at her and was about to introduce myself, but she wasn't paying attention to me. I looked around the classroom, trying to make eye contact. No one else was really paying attention to me either.

I looked at the yellow paper again. *Third, fifth, and seventh periods—worksheets 13A and 13B. Walk fourth period to lunch at 11:35. Sixth period planning.* Was that it? I flipped the paper over, expecting to find more information on the back. It was blank.

Fumbling around the desk a bit more revealed worksheets 12A, 13A, and 13B. I put them in three neat stacks and shoved everything else to the side.

As kids continued to trickle in, I walked to the front of the room. I wrote my name on the blackboard and stood grinning at no one in particular.

Steve thought substitute teaching would probably be easy for me. "After all," he'd said, "you've got years of experience dealing with our kids all day long." But now, standing in front of a room filled with twelve-year-olds, armed with nothing but scribbled instructions and a few math worksheets, I could already see that this was very different from being a mom.

There were so many kids. They were so loud. They were so big. And worse, they were strangers. At least with my own kids I could tell when Angela was lying. And when Danny was acting insane—because he was tired—I knew that dunking him into a warm bath with a couple toy boats would solve all our problems. But I didn't even know any of these kids' first names, let alone a single thing about them or who they were or what they were like. Not to mention the fact that dunking any of them into a warm bath was definitely not an option.

The bell rang.

"Good morning," I said. Despite my best efforts, my voice was slightly shaking. "I'm Mrs. Hershey."

"Where's Mrs. Thompson?" a boy in the third row yelled.

"I don't know," I said. "But she left this assignment for you." I suddenly realized I'd been clutching the stack of worksheets against my chest like some sort of protective shield. I started passing them out.

"Can I go to the bathroom?" someone called out.

"The bathroom?" I repeated. Was there some sort of policy about that? Was I allowed to let them leave the room? "Well …" I tried to remember if this had been addressed during orientation, but I couldn't remember anything like that being discussed. There was certainly nothing useful in the way of classroom rules and procedures on that sheet of yellow paper. "Do you need me to write you a hall pass or something?"

"It's over there!" yelled almost half the class as they pointed at a green plastic stick hanging from the blackboard. *HALL PASS* was written on it in black.

"Oh," I said. "Well, sure. If that's how you do it, then go ahead."

A boy with shaggy brown hair leaped out of his seat. He was wearing a Pink Floyd T-shirt. The boy grabbed the hall pass and left the room, letting the door slam behind him.

"Hey, this worksheet is hard!" someone shouted from the right side of the room. "I don't even know how to do number one!"

"What are you, stupid?" yelled someone from the left side of the room.

"We never learned how to do this!" came a third voice.

"Yeah we did. We just did it yesterday, remember? You cross multiply, so it'd be twenty times x …"

"Oh yeah. Okay, now I remember."

"Hey, can I go to the bathroom?"

"Parker already went!"

"Well, can I go when he comes back?"

"Hey!" came an indignant voice from the back row. "Will everyone shut up? I'm trying to learn!"

Laughter erupted all over the room.

I straightened up and cleared my throat. "Okay everybody, it's time to be quiet and get to work." I was trying to look and sound authoritative. "If you have a question, please raise your hand and I'll come over to your desk. If you need to go to the bathroom, you don't have to ask, just quietly take the hall pass and go." I took two steps toward the desks and slowly gazed around the room. I was hoping it would make me seem a bit more formidable.

Two girls in the back row leaned toward each other, whispered something, and giggled. The rest of the class got to work, or at least pretended to.

The shaggy-haired boy returned from the bathroom, letting the door slam behind him. He hung up the hall pass and sauntered back to his seat.

Two boys from different sides of the classroom instantly sprinted toward the front. They simultaneously grabbed for the hall pass.

"I had it first!" one of them yelled, trying to wrestle the pass out of the other boy's hand.

"Yeah, but I have to go more than you do!" the other boy said, tugging back.

The class laughed.

"All right," I said, "you in the green shirt, you had it first, so go ahead. If we have any more fights over the hall pass no one gets to leave for the rest of the period. And please don't let the door slam …"

Green Shirt strode out of the room. The door slammed behind him.

The loser in the hall pass skirmish shrugged and went back to his seat. "Whatever," he said. "Just don't be surprised if there's a yellow puddle on the floor."

"Eww!" a girl yelled, throwing her pencil down on the desk. "That's gross Dylan!"

"I'm just sayin'." He shrugged again, picked up his pencil, and scribbled something at the top of his worksheet.

Except for the sounds of pencils on paper and a skinny kid with glasses in the second row who kept coughing, the room was quiet for a couple minutes. I didn't really know what I was supposed to do at that point, so I slowly walked up and down the rows like some sort of security guard.

Green Shirt came back and the door banged behind him. He hung up the hall pass and went to his seat.

Nobody seemed to need my help solving problems using ratios and proportions. It was just as well, as I wasn't sure I could've helped them anyway. I sighed and looked at the clock. Okay, almost thirty-five minutes left in the period, I thought.

I headed back to the teacher's desk. I was debating whether or not I should start writing notes about the day for Mrs. Thompson, like they'd told us to do during the orientation. Of course, I didn't really have much to report. I suppose I could inform her that there was a strange epidemic of students needing to use the bathroom, I thought.

A short freckle-faced boy materialized in front of me.

"I'm done," he said, waving his paper in the air. "What do I do now?"

"You're done already?"

"Yeah." He looked a little puzzled as to why I would be surprised that he was finished. "So what do I do?"

That was a good question. I picked up the yellow sheet of instructions and flipped it over in case new writing had magically appeared on the back. Unfortunately, it had not.

I had no idea what to do. Was I supposed to collect the assignment? Grade it? Was it possible that there was an answer key buried somewhere on the desk? Should I just tell him to stuff it in his math folder and bring it back to class tomorrow?

I jumped as the door slammed again. As soon as the hall pass was hung back up, a girl with a blond ponytail skipped to the front of the room, snatched the pass, and headed out. *Bam*!

"Uh, if you're done, I'll take your work," I said to the freckle-faced kid. "I guess … I guess you can just work on homework for another class."

"I don't have any," he said.

"Oh, well then, I guess you can read."

"I don't have a book."

"Okay, well … just find something to do," I said, waving him away.

"What do we do when we're done?" asked a girl in the second row. She was holding her paper in the air.

I shot a glance at the clock, then back at her. "You're done already too?"

"Yeah. There were only, like, twenty problems," she said.

The girl with the blond ponytail came bouncing back into the room. The door slammed behind her.

"Listen!" I said. "Could everybody please not let the door slam …"

A girl got up from the front row, grabbed the hall pass, and slipped out the door. *Bang!*

This is obviously a losing battle, I thought.

I turned to the class. "Okay, if you finish early, bring your papers up to me. No, wait. Put them … put them in a pile on this table," I said, walking over to a round table in the front corner of the room. "And then you can read or do homework for another …"

I was practically knocked over by the deluge of seventh graders rushing to the front of the room to drop their work on the table. Instead of the pile I was hoping for, it looked like the table had been turned into some sort of abstract art involving math papers.

"*All* of you are done?" I asked, looking at the clock in a panic.

"Sure, it was easy," said a girl with curly hair, tossing her paper toward the table. It fluttered onto the floor as she turned and walked back to her seat.

"Um, I think you missed," I said. "Come pick your paper up, um, uh …" It was so hard to talk to these kids when I didn't even know their names. "Um … girl with the curly hair! Come back!"

"That's Nicole," another girl said, throwing her own paper down on the abstract art design.

"Thank you," I said. "Nicole, could you …"

Bam! Someone else returned from the bathroom.

A boy stepped on Nicole's paper as he walked back to his seat.

"Nicole, could you please come pick up your paper and put it on the table?" I said.

Nicole looked like she didn't know what I was talking about. Then she yelled, "Hey Tori, can you pick my paper up off the floor?"

"Yeah, sure," said Tori, scooping up the paper—which was now half-crumpled and marred by a sneaker print—and flinging it on the table.

When the flurry had settled down and the kids were back in their seats I began turning the math paper tablecloth into a neat stack. It gave me something to do, at least.

I still had over fifteen minutes before these kids left and a fresh crop arrived. What was this Mrs. Thompson person thinking? Did she really think that one lousy worksheet was enough to keep these kids busy for nearly an hour?

When I was finished straightening the papers I looked around. One boy had folded up a sheet of paper and was getting ready to fly it across the room. Another was repeatedly kicking the chair in front of him. This caused the occupant of the chair to whip around and yell, "Quit it!"

The noise level seemed to be increasing by the second. There were no less than five different conversations going on, one of which was being had by four boys in the back of the room sitting on top of their desks.

"Everyone needs to find something to do!" I announced over the commotion.

The boy with the paper airplane took careful aim and shot it across the room.

"Don't you have any homework for another class you can work on?" I pleaded. "Or a book you can read? Or something?"

"Nope," said one of the boys who was perched on top of his desk.

"Well, then you need to …"

A tall boy in baggy jeans came back in the room. *Bam*! He hung up the hall pass and went to his seat.

"Would everybody please stop letting the door slam!" I said.

A girl with a pink headband and matching pink lip gloss rolled her eyes and pressed her lips together, trying to mask her laughter. And a boy muttered, "Crazy lady."

I ignored them and pointed at a boy who'd grabbed the hall pass and was reaching for the door. "No," I said. "No more. Sit down."

He looked at me and hesitated.

"Sit!"

He carefully hung up the hall pass and shuffled back to his seat.

"Nobody else is leaving the room till the bell rings!" I barked.

"But I have to …"

"No!" I said. "You can wait fifteen minutes. Now I want everybody to sit in their chairs, not on the desks, and find something quiet to do that doesn't bother anybody else!"

The boys in the back glared at me before slowly sliding down into their seats. The girl who'd been trying to hide her laughter by pursing her lips had to resort to covering her mouth with her hand.

Everybody sat quietly at their desks for the next ten minutes. Of course, this was probably because I was walking up and down the rows, watching them like a hawk.

Five minutes before class was over, everybody suddenly began packing up—it was as if a silent alarm had gone off. Kids were scooping up books and notebooks from under their chairs and slamming them on the desks. Backpacks being zipped open and shut sounded all over the room. Then, everyone seemed to scoot their rear end to the edge of their seat until they were balancing on about the last quarter inch.

Next thing I knew, about half the class exploded into conversation. Fine, I thought. Let them talk. I give up. As long as no one gets hurt, I guess they can do whatever they want.

The bell rang. Everyone sprang out of their seats and to the door so quickly that there was a traffic jam in the doorway.

As the last few students headed out, I looked around the room. The floor was covered with three wadded balls of paper, two flat sheets of paper, at least four pencils of various sizes, and one battered copy of *The Giver*. For some unknown reason, two chairs were on their sides.

I was debating whether to straighten everything up or just leave it all when a fresh batch of kids started wandering in. I faced the door, smiled, and tried to look like I knew what I was doing.

A boy stopped and studied me. "Your front tooth is crooked," he informed me before walking toward his desk.

My smile faded. I ran my tongue over my front teeth as he strode away.

"Hey, Miss, uh … Sub Lady!" someone yelled. "Can I go to the bathroom before class starts?"

It's going to be a long day, I thought.

By 11:35 a.m. it felt like an eternity had passed. It was finally time to walk fourth period to lunch. After being locked in a room all morning—with various groups of raucous people—the idea of spending thirty minutes in a quiet room by myself while I munched on the ham sandwich and bag of Fritos that were tucked in my purse sounded like heaven.

We walked down two hallways and into the huge cafeteria, trying not to get run over by the students who were rushing in the opposite direction. I waited a minute or two to make sure the whole class arrived safely. Once I was certain that I was no longer needed, I turned and walked toward the cafeteria door as quickly as I could without actually breaking into a sprint like I wanted to.

As I was about to step into the hallway, I heard a voice sharply say, "Where are you going?"

I turned around expecting to see a kid getting in trouble for something. Instead, a thin woman with glasses and a stern face was looking right at me.

"Well," I said, a little confused, "I was just going to head back to the classroom to have my lunch." Then I realized that maybe that wasn't the norm for most teachers. "Oh, is there a teacher's lounge where all the seventh grade teachers sit together? Thanks so much for the invite, but I think today I'd just prefer to ..."

"Aren't you the sub for Mrs. Thompson?" she interrupted.

"Yes." I smiled. "I'm Heather Hershey. This is my first day here."

The woman didn't return my smile. "Didn't she tell you?"

"Tell me what?" I was getting the feeling this wasn't a lunch invitation after all.

She gave an exasperated sigh. "The seventh grade teachers rotate silent lunch duty. Today is Mrs. Thompson's day, and since you're her sub, that means it's you."

I blinked a couple times. "I'm sorry. What?"

"Silent lunch!" she bellowed at me, gesturing toward a table on a raised platform against the left wall of the cafeteria. About eight kids were sitting at the table. "The students who have silent lunch need an adult to monitor them, and today that adult is you."

My eyes darted over to the silent lunch table. "You mean I have to spend my lunch break sitting at a table with all the kids who got in trouble?"

"That's right," she said curtly.

I eyed the table again. One of the silent lunch boys laughed loudly and shoved the boy sitting next to him.

"And what do I, uh ... do, exactly?"

"You make sure they stay silent," she said. "Now you'd better hurry up. You're already late."

I gulped as she walked away. Then I made my way over to the table of troublemakers.

I stood looking at them for a moment. It felt as though I had to oversee some sort of strange board meeting of sulky twelve-year-olds. "Ahem," I said to the hoodlums, "I'm Mrs. Hershey, and I'll be, uh ... joining you for silent lunch today."

They stared at me and continued chewing.

I carefully eyed the kids—as if they were predators possibly about to attack at any minute—as I sat down. Unfortunately, I was watching them instead of looking at what I was doing and I ended up missing my chair. I had to clutch the edge of the table to keep from sliding right down and plopping onto the floor of the delinquent diner.

There was a collective outburst of snickers and snorts as the group of lunch exiles exchanged glances. I pretended nothing had happened and focused on unwrapping my ham sandwich. Of course, I no longer had much of an appetite.

Hopefully I'll start booking a lot of weddings *really* soon, I thought.

Twelve

"Okay, kids," I announced as I hung up the phone, "everybody go to the bathroom and then put on some shoes. I have to meet with a bride who's considering hiring me, and you're coming along."

I walked down the hall to my bedroom. I yanked open my dresser drawer and grabbed a pair of pantyhose, slipping my hand into one leg to check for runs.

Angela appeared in the doorway. "Does she want to meet us too?" she asked eagerly.

"No." The pantyhose had a huge run. I flung them across the room and took out another pair. Luckily, they passed the check. "You're coming because Daddy just called and said he has an emergency at work and has to stay late and I can't get a babysitter on such short notice." I slammed the drawer shut and started rooting around the closet for a dress. "Danny! Are you getting ready? We have to go somewhere!" I held up two dresses and showed them to Angela. "Which one is better, the brown or the green?"

"Green," Angela said. "It matches your eyes."

"Got it." I hung the brown dress up and threw the green one across my bed.

"Danny, did you hear me?" I yelled. "We have to go in a couple minutes!"

"I'll get him." Angela skipped out of the room.

I took off my jeans and sweatshirt. Then I sat on the bed to pull on my pantyhose.

Dragging my kids along to meet with a prospective client is crazy, I thought. What respectable business owner does that?

Unfortunately, I didn't have a choice. I'd called Bridget, the bride, as soon as I'd gotten off the phone with Steve. I explained to her that I needed to reschedule, but she insisted that we go ahead and meet this evening. She lived in Indiana—or Illinois, I forget which—and said she would only be in town for a couple days. "It's no problem to bring them," she assured me. "I don't mind. I love kids."

"Danny!" Angela screamed.

I pulled the green dress over my head and wiggled it into position. I could hear the kids in Danny's room.

"You're supposed to be getting ready to go, not sitting there playing," Angela said. "Now give me those trucks and go put your shoes on."

I reached into the bathroom drawer for my hairbrush and started running it through my hair.

"Hey!" Danny shouted. "Gimme back my trucks!"

"Not until you've put your shoes on," said Angela.

I tossed my hairbrush back in the drawer and hurried to put on a bit of makeup.

"I said gimme!" Danny screeched.

"No!" Angela yelled. "First put your shoes on."

Here it comes, any second now, I thought.

"Mahh-meeeee!!!" Angela shrieked. "Danny whacked me!"

And there it was. I scooped up my purse and the Manila folder with the paperwork for Bridget's wedding and headed down the hall. Angela was standing on her tiptoes, holding two Matchbox trucks above her head. Danny was furiously jumping up, trying to reach them.

"Angela," I said, "why don't you just worry about yourself. I'll take care of Danny."

"Fine," said Angela, tossing the trucks at Danny's feet.

He quickly snatched them up and glared at her.

I glanced at my watch. "Angela, if you're ready, go ahead and get in the car. Danny, go get your shoes on. You can bring your trucks with you if you want. Just hurry, both of you!"

Danny tugged on his second shoe and both kids stumbled out the door. I grabbed a couple coloring books and a box of crayons off the coffee table and stuffed them in my purse before following the kids toward the car.

I wondered if Bridget would still love children after today.

*   *   *

As soon as we walked into the coffee shop, a woman with dark curly hair approached me. She was holding a cup of coffee with a lid.

"You must be Heather," she said. "I recognize you from your photo on the website."

"That's me," I said as I shook her hand. "And you must be Bridget. So nice to meet you. Congratulations on your engagement."

"Thank you." Bridget motioned toward an older woman next to her who was wearing designer glasses, a gold and sapphire necklace, and a lavender pantsuit. "This is my mother, Grace Reese."

"Oh!" I was surprised. I had no idea that I'd also be meeting with a mother of the bride, let alone one who looked like an executive. I extended my hand a second time. "Nice to meet you, Grace."

"It's Ms. Reese," she said coolly as she weakly shook my hand.

I gulped. "Ms. Reese, of course. So nice to meet you."

"And who are they?" asked Ms. Reese with a sweeping gesture.

I turned around. Angela was having a particularly frizzy hair day, even for her. She was shoving Danny and I suddenly noticed the ketchup stain on his shirt—and that he'd put his shoes on the wrong feet.

"These are my two children." I took Angela's offending hand and gave it a gentle squeeze. "Danny and Angela."

I thought I saw Grace—I mean, *Ms. Reese*—recoil ever so slightly.

"Charmed," she finally said.

"Oh, they are so cute!" Bridget gushed.

"They wouldn't be coming with me to the wedding, of course," I said, attempting to make a joke and laughing nervously. The way Ms. Reese was looking at me was making me very uneasy.

"No, I would certainly hope not," said Ms. Reese, frowning as she stared at Danny.

I shot my eyes in his direction. He was working his right index finger up his nose. I let go of Angela's hand and quickly tugged Danny's right arm toward me in what I hoped looked like an affectionate gesture.

"Well," Bridget chirped, clasping her hands and apparently oblivious to any nose-picking going in her vicinity, "let's all go have a seat."

We walked through the coffee shop and stopped at an empty booth with a small table next to it.

"Here," I said, setting the crayons and coloring books down on the small table, "you kids sit here while we adults talk at the other table."

"Can I have a muffin?" Danny asked as he sat down.

"Ooh, and can I have one of those milkshake things?" Angela pointed to a woman who was sitting at a table by the window. She had some sort of frozen mocha drink with whipped cream.

Danny jerked his head around to see what Angela was pointing at. "Oh yeah!" he yelled, whipping his finger toward it. "I want one of those too!"

The woman looked up from her book and right at us.

I gave her a polite smile and turned back to the kids. "First of all, please don't point," I said quietly. "Second, that's not a milkshake. It's an adult coffee drink that probably costs a fortune. And anyway," I growled, leaning in closer, "we're not here to eat. We're here for me to do business. Remember?"

"But I'm really really thirsty," Danny whined. "Can't I just get something to drink?"

"Yeah, me too," Angela chimed in. "Can't we please get sodas? Please?"

I took a deep breath. I realized that time and money spent getting two small Cokes would be a worthwhile investment to buy me the peace and quiet I needed to get through this meeting successfully.

I smiled sweetly at Bridget and her mother. "Excuse me just a moment." I walked up to the counter and placed my order.

"Yay! Thank you Mommy!" Angela squealed as I put two drinks with lids and two straws down on their table.

"You're welcome," I said. "Now listen, I need you guys to sit quietly and not pester me or fight, okay? So why don't you both just color and enjoy your sodas?"

Before the kids could argue with me, I sat down opposite Bridget and her mother. "Thank you for waiting." I opened my Manila folder. "Now, my notes from our phone call the other day say that you want me to play for the ceremony only, and that it's an outdoor wedding at Edgewood Gardens so I would need to bring my keyboard. Is that correct?"

"That's right," said Bridget, "but we also want music before the ceremony begins."

"No problem," I said, finally starting to relax a little. "My ceremony package includes thirty minutes of prelude music while the guests are ..."

Danny appeared approximately six inches away from my face. "I'm done."

"Excuse me," I said to Bridget and her mother. I flashed them another sweet smile before turning to Danny. "What do you mean, you're done?" I whispered.

"I'm done coloring," he said.

I glanced at the small table. Angela was carefully outlining a princess dress in yellow and Danny's picture of a monster truck had a few scribbles of red across it. "Okay."

Ms. Reese leaned over and said something to Bridget.

"Then just find another picture in the book to color," I said to Danny.

"But I'm bored with coloring," Danny said.

Ms. Reese was still talking to Bridget in a hushed voice. This was not good.

"Fine," I said, "then play with the trucks you brought."

"What trucks?"

My eyes flitted over to Bridget and her mother, then back to Danny. "You were playing with some trucks right before we left," I said through clenched teeth. "I told you to bring them."

Danny looked puzzled. "You did?"

Angela looked up from her princess picture. "You didn't tell him to bring them. You told him he *could* bring them if he wanted to."

"Yeah!" Danny looked like he still had no idea what was going on, but he was happy to hear that he was somehow right.

"Thank you, Angela," I said grimly.

"Sure!" she squeaked as she went back to coloring.

Ms. Reese grimaced at me. "Perhaps we should do this another time," she said sharply.

"Oh no, Mom!" Bridget cried. She looked hurt. "My flight home is tomorrow afternoon, and anyway, we're all here right now. It'd be silly to leave."

"Perhaps we should consider other options," Ms. Reese murmured to Bridget. "Remember how we talked earlier about possibly hiring a string quartet?"

Bridget shook her head quickly. "Oh no. I really want to have piano music. And anyway, a string quartet is so much more expensive."

"We have the money," Ms. Reese told her.

She said that a little too quickly, I thought.

"Mom!" Bridget hissed, jerking her head in my direction.

"Well, fine then, if that's what you want," Ms. Reese said with a sigh.

"Yes, it is." Bridget smiled at me, looking a little embarrassed. "Go on, Heather. What were you saying?"

At that point, I had no idea what I'd been saying. But Danny had drifted back to his table and he was coloring again, so I figured I'd better say something, anything, while I still had the chance.

"Have you decided what music you'd like to walk down the aisle to?" I asked.

Bridget thought for a moment. "I think I'll go with the Bridal March. I like how it …"

"Mahh-meee!" Angela yelled. "Danny's peeling all the crayons!"

"Excuse me," I faintly muttered to Bridget as I slid out of the booth.

"Danny's ruining all the crayons!" said Angela. "He's peeling off the wrappers!"

"You can still use them," Danny said, picking at the Blizzard Blue with his fingernail.

"Cut it out!" Angela screeched.

I put my palms down on the table and leaned in so close that my nose was practically touching Angela's. "Look," I whispered fiercely, "you two sit here quietly and leave us alone for fifteen minutes, or I will find a creative way to make the rest of your week very, very unpleasant."

They both stared at me in shock.

"What? What did I do?" Danny moaned.

"Yeah!" said Angela. She was suddenly on Danny's side. "What are you yelling at us for?"

"All we're doing is sitting here!" Danny exclaimed.

"Yeah!" Angela said with a sharp nod of her head.

I took a deep breath as I tried to remember how cute they both were when they were babies. It didn't help. "Do not fight," I whispered through clenched teeth, "or bother me. Or else."

"Cheez, what's wrong with her?" Danny asked Angela as I slinked back into the booth.

"Thank you for being so patient," I said to Bridget and her mother, putting on my sweetest smile, yet again.

"Oh, no problem," said Bridget with a little flip of her fingers. "They're both so adorable."

Ms. Reese said nothing. But she kept her eyes focused on me as she took a long sip of coffee.

"Thank you." I was grateful that, so far at least, Bridget thought my two little sidekicks were amusing. "All right then, so you would like the traditional Bridal March." I picked up my pen and wrote a note on the contract. "And you had mentioned in our phone conversation that you want Jesu, Joy of Man's Desiring for the processional and Ode to Joy for the recessional, and that there is no interlude music. Is that still correct?"

"Uh-huh," Bridget said.

"All right, so we have all your music choices. Do you have any questions for me?"

Bridget glanced at her mom then shook her head. "No, I think we're good."

"Okay, then. I think that's everything." I turned the contract around and laid it down on the table in front of them. "Go ahead and look this over and let me know if you have any questions."

Bridget picked up the contract and moved her lips slightly as she read it to herself. "Okay, this looks great." She put the contract down. "So now do I just sign this and write you a check?"

"Yes," I said, breathing a quiet sigh of relief. "A fifty percent deposit is requested to secure the date, and then the remaining balance will be due on …"

Angela shrieked. Out of the corner of my eye I saw a plastic cup about three feet in the air above the kids. It landed with an explosion of soda and ice cubes that splashed all over the small table and floor. And, of course, one ice cube bounced up and hit the edge of our table with a graceful spin.

"Excuse me," I squeaked to Bridget and her mother as I jumped up to get some napkins.

"What just happened?" I barked at the kids as I threw handfuls of napkins over the drenched table.

Danny grinned. He was oblivious to—or maybe proud of—the havoc he'd caused. "I wanted to see if the cup would fall off if I picked it up by the lid."

"And I guess you found out." I grabbed a napkin and frantically used it to scoop the ice up off the floor.

"Are we leaving soon?" Angela was looking around. "I'm bored."

"Yeah, and can I get another soda?" Danny asked.

"Don't … talk … to me … right now," I growled as I grabbed the soggy napkins off the table and carried them over to the trash can.

I went back to my table. Ms. Reese was sullenly inspecting her sleeve for soda spatter, and I braced myself for the worst. I knew I was lucky that Bridget had hung in there for so long. But I had no doubt that any chance of getting this job went flying out the window the instant the drink went flying out of Danny's hand.

"Here ya go," Bridget said, handing me the signed contract.

I took it from her, speechless.

"Mom's writing the check." Bridget gestured toward Ms. Reese who was writing with a gold-plated pen.

I stared at Bridget's signature at the bottom of the contract and blinked a couple times.

"Is something wrong?" Bridget leaned forward and peered over the contract. "Did I sign it in the wrong spot or something?"

"Nope!" I said happily, glancing down at the contract then back up at Bridget. "Nope, this is perfect!" A little laugh fluttered out of me as I opened my folder and took out the duplicate contract. "And here's your copy."

Ms. Reese finished writing the check, tore it off, and handed it to me. I wasn't positive, but I thought I had to give it an extra little tug before she finally let go.

"Thank you both so much," I said, quickly getting up and gathering my things. I knew I'd better usher the human tornadoes out of there before they caused some other disaster and Ms. Reese would have no choice but to lean forward, pluck the check and signed contract out of my hands, and rip them up. "I'll be in touch about all the details the week before the wedding. But in the meantime, don't hesitate to contact me." I put a hand on each kid's back and started herding them toward the door.

"Thank you so much for taking the time to meet with us," said Bridget. She tilted her head and flipped her fingers in a little wave. "Bye kids! Nice meeting you!"

Angela turned around and grinned. "We've never been to a wedding before. So do you think we could …"

"Bye!" I yelled quickly, spinning Angela back around and steering her and Danny out the door.

"Did you get the job?" Angela asked once we were outside.

"Amazingly, yes," I said.

"I'd really like to go to the wedding with you," she said hopefully. "Can I?"

I clutched the envelope containing the proof of my success closer to my chest. "Ha ha. Yeah, I don't think so."

Thirteen

Bridget's wedding venue was beautiful. Edgewood Gardens was a historic white house—complete with pillars—on the outskirts of the metro area. It was nestled back in a grove, and not even visible from the main road.

There was a huge patio behind the house. It was filled with rows of white wooden chairs decorated with purple sash bows, pink roses, and baby's breath. The chairs were facing a gazebo with strings of hanging lights and plenty of room for me to set up my keyboard in the back corner.

Even though I couldn't help feeling a little nervous, I was confident that this would definitely not be a repeat of Christine's church wedding. For one thing, I'd purchased and learned plenty of new music for the prelude and could probably keep playing for an hour and a half if I had to. And for another thing, I met the wedding coordinator as soon as I arrived and she seemed like a very competent woman. She knew what was going on, and she immediately knew who I was. She showed me exactly where the bridal party would be entering and where she would be standing to give me the music cues.

I played through the prelude music, the mothers' entrance, and then the song for the bridesmaids. Each song gave me a sense of growing confidence. I was experienced. I was prepared. I was …

Doot doot deedle-eet!

Huh?

Doot doot deedle-eet!! Doot doot …

Oh no. Oh no no no no no. I knew that sound. It was my cell phone. It was in my purse which was on the floor under the keyboard, near my left foot.

… deedle-eet!

There was no way I could reach it from where I was sitting. I started swinging my left foot around—which is not easy to do when you're pedaling with your right foot—to try to kick it closer while still keeping an eye on the bridesmaids coming down the aisle.

Doot doot …

Got it! If I just leeeeaned to the left, I could stop playing with my left hand for just a second while I reeeeeached …

My phone stopped. I kept playing and slowly got back into an upright position.

Meanwhile, the fifth and final bridesmaids approached their spots. I quickly whipped the music book off the keyboard and slapped three pages of Wager's Bridal March into place.

As Bridget started down the path behind the white chairs the guests stood up and turned toward her. She was wearing a beautiful A-line gown with a dipped neckline, and she looked radiant.

Just then, a breeze stirred. The edges of my music pages fluttered. Uh-oh, I thought.

Bridget turned at the end of the path and began walking down the aisle.

Flutter, flutter, flutter. I pushed my left hand against the pages and tried playing with just my right hand, but that obviously wasn't going to work.

Bridget was almost halfway down the aisle.

Please, please, no more wind, I thought. Just please give me thirty breezeless seconds, and then there can be huge gusts of wind all over the place. There can be a freaking tornado during the ceremony for all I care. Just please, please, please, let me finish.

Another breeze rose up. Oh no no no no no no!

WHOOOSH! All three pages went flying into the air.

I frantically reached up to grab them, but they seemed to have minds of their own as they flapped around in all directions. Despite my best efforts, they danced happily out of the gazebo and tumbled across the lawn, never to be seen again.

I of course had to keep playing after the mass exodus of my music. So I fumbled around in the same key as best I could, trying to play a melody that sounded semi-accurate until Bridget mercifully arrived at the altar.

"Friends and family of Bridget and Alex," the officiant said, "welcome, and thank you for being here on this important day."

Well, what do you know. I wasn't as prepared as I thought I was.

Fourteen

"It was awful," I said to Steve that evening as I told him the whole story. "I was so embarrassed, and I had to sit right there where everybody could stare at me during the entire ceremony. I'm sure they were all thinking I was a total idiot."

"Hmm." Steve thought for a moment. "I know what you need to do. Create a checklist on your phone for everything you need to do before a wedding. Make sure it includes putting all your music in a three-ring binder and packing some clips. Then, the last thing on your list should be turning off your phone. That way, this won't happen again." He picked up the TV remote and went back to watching an episode of *Star Trek*.

"Thanks," I mumbled.

Men—all solution, no sympathy.

* * *

Later that week I was talking to Stephanie on the phone. "It was horrendous," I said. "I was completely mortified.

I had to sit in plain view of everybody through the whole ceremony. And they could stare at me after my stupid phone went off and my music blew away. I'm positive they all thought I was a total idiot."

"Oh, I'm sure they weren't thinking about you," she said. "It was a wedding. Everybody probably had their eyes on the bride and was just thinking about how beautiful she looked and what a happy couple they were. I bet most people didn't even notice."

"Maybe." I still wasn't convinced.

"And even if they *did* notice, they probably thought it was kind of funny seeing all the papers suddenly go flying away like that. I know I would've thought it was funny."

"I guess." I was trying to imagine if it could've been funny to anyone other than her.

"So think of it this way," she said, "you gave a couple guests a funny story to tell about the wedding the next day. Everybody needs a good funny wedding story, right?"

"Well, that's one way of looking at it." I chuckled.

"But really, I doubt most people even noticed. I wouldn't worry about it. Anyway, you should be really excited. You've played for two weddings now. You're getting to be a real pro."

She was right. It was two more weddings than I'd played for six months ago. That was exciting. See, this is why God created girlfriends, I thought.

The next day Bridget sent a very nice email thanking me and telling me that the music was beautiful. That was the important thing—the bride was happy. So I tried not to worry about it.

* * *

A few nights later Steve sighed as he came into the kitchen. "All right. I think I finally got them both to bed. We finished a chapter of *Mrs. Piggle-Wiggle*, everybody went to the bathroom, and Danny has Bunny-Bun. What's up?"

"I'm trying to figure out what to cook this week." I was leaning against the counter looking up recipes on my phone. "How does chicken broccoli casserole sound?"

"Sounds great." He grabbed an apple from the fruit bowl. "It's been nice to have some real food around here. Thank you."

"You should try cooking with me sometime," I said as I went to the fridge. "It's not as hard as I thought. It's actually a little fun." I scrolled down to the list of ingredients. "Let's see, do we have mayonnaise?" I put my phone on the counter and started going through the stuff in the door shelves. "Ranch dressing, tartar sauce … eww, this looks really old." I leaned over and threw it in the trash.

My phone made a binging sound.

"You got an email," Steve said. "You want me to check it?"

"Yeah, sure." Aha, there was mayonnaise. I opened the jar just to make sure we had enough, then checked the expiration date. Yup, that will work, I thought.

"It's a notification for a review posted on your profile."

I shut the fridge and walked over to him. "What is that? Spam?"

"I dunno. It says it's from Wedding Wild."

"Wedding Wild?" I repeated. "Why are they … oh! I know what it is. Someone must've left a review on my page. Ooh, how exciting." I started bouncing up and down on my toes. "Who's it from? What does it say?"

Steve leaned against the counter and clicked the link. His eyes narrowed. After a couple more seconds, he frowned. "Hmm."

I stopped bouncing. "*Hmm*? What does *hmm* mean?"

Steve kept frowning at the phone.

I was getting nervous. "What? What is it? They said something bad, didn't they?"

Steve looked at me and opened his mouth as if to say something. Then he pressed his lips together.

I was stunned. Why would either of my two brides be logging into the website to write bad things about me? Sure, everything wasn't perfect, but overall things went fairly well. When all was said and done, both brides seemed very happy. And anyway, why would a new bride be pounding out mean, negative posts about the people who were part of *the happiest day of her life*? Weren't they supposed to be joyously honeymooning and sorting through all their expensive wedding gifts and … well, just busy being in a constant state of marital bliss?

"What does it say?" I asked, although the idea of actually finding out made me feel ill.

He handed me the phone and I forced myself to look.

I was very disappointed to have Heather Hershey play at my daughter's wedding ceremony last week.

Of course. Bridget's *mother* wrote the nasty review. She wasn't in a state of starry-eyed marital bliss. She wasn't busy writing thank you notes, sorting photos of her honeymoon, and happily arranging all her new china and fondue sets. She was just as grumpy and whiny as the rest of us. Not to mention, she obviously disliked me from the get-go and was probably actively looking for things I did wrong that day—not that she had to look very hard.

"I don't believe this," I muttered.

I suspected that we were not dealing with a true professional when my daughter and I met with Mrs. Hershey for a consultation and she not only brought along her two unruly children, but spent most of the time unsuccessfully attempting to discipline them. Unfortunately, my suspicions were confirmed when Mrs. Hershey's phone went off during the ceremony and ruined the special moment for myself, my daughter, and all our guests. As if that weren't enough, her music went flying off the piano during my daughter's entrance, creating a huge spectacle and embarrassing us all.

Unfortunately, there was more. My stomach tightened and I started feeling dizzy. I put my hand on the edge of the counter.

I urge anybody hiring a wedding pianist to not make the same mistake we did, and to be sure to hire somebody who is professional and has plenty of experience – neither of which is true about Heather Hershey.

I took a few steps toward the kitchen table. It felt like I was moving in slow motion. I sank into a chair and buried my head in hands.

This horrible, sick feeling felt distinctly familiar. For a few seconds I couldn't figure out why, but then it was obvious. It felt like I was right back in that small room almost fifteen years ago …

*   *   *

"You don't have to, Heather," Dr. Adams said gently. "You're welcome to finish the year with us and see if you pass your sophomore technical exam. But … it might be, well … *easier* for you to start thinking about other options now."

My throat tightened so much that I felt like I could barely breathe, never mind speak. I watched my hands trembling in my lap.

I knew what this was all about. Yesterday morning I'd played Bach's Prelude and Fugue in D Major and had a complete memory glitch during the fugue. I kept getting stuck and circling back to the same spot until I finally gave up and just finished the piece and walked off the stage.

It was embarrassing, but I wasn't expecting this. I sat studying my trembling hands.

"I know this is a lot to take in," said Dr. Adams. "Why don't we go ahead and skip your lesson today? Just relax and take some time to think about it. You don't need to make any decisions right now. The registrar's office will let you fill out the change of degree application at any time."

I might have mumbled a thank you as I gathered my books and stumbled out of the room. I made my way down the hall to the nearest bathroom and checked to make sure it was empty before I locked myself in a stall and sobbed.

A week later I filled out the application to change my major to business. I chose business because it sounded both practical and like the polar opposite of piano performance.

After that, I never set foot in the music building of Johnston College ever again.

*   *   *

I looked down. My hands were trembling on the kitchen table.

"What am I going to do?" I whispered. "Everybody who looks for a wedding pianist on Wedding Wild is going to see this. No one will ever call me again. It's over ... I barely even started, and it's over."

Steve walked over to the table and sat down next to me.

"Can you delete your profile?" he asked quietly.

I let my hands slide into my lap, then stared in a daze at a spot of peeling wallpaper. "I guess ..." I mumbled. "But what's worse, not being listed at all, or having a listing that says awful things?"

I went to bed early that night and didn't take the sub job I was called for the next morning. I deleted my Wedding Wild profile and stayed in my pajamas until 11 a.m.

I finally got showered and dressed. I sat down on the piano bench. Instead of playing, I just sat there and stared at the keys. I had no desire to play. I had no desire to do anything. After sitting there for several minutes, I put away my music, closed the lid, and tucked in the bench.

I grabbed the TV remote and flopped down on the couch. I stayed there for the next two hours.

Fifteen

Over the next few weeks I found myself taking on more substitute teaching jobs. Pretty soon I was working almost every day.

The more I did it, the easier it became—although some classes were bumpier than others. I got to know a few of the kids' names, and I was figuring out how to get their attention and keep things moving along. Most importantly, I learned that a roomful of kids with nothing to do was the kiss of death for a substitute teacher. So I compiled a big binder of word searches, crossword puzzles, and other worksheets that I could whip out if necessary.

Some days I was bored out of my mind, like the day I sat through a science documentary about organelles and mitosis five times. But some days were a little fun, and luckily, I never had silent lunch duty again.

One day a sixth grade class had to read a couple chapters of *Roll of Thunder, Hear My Cry* and answer questions about it. I took the liberty of reading the chapters out loud and discussing the questions with the class. I guess the years of reading to Danny and Angela made me pretty good at it, because I managed to hold everybody's attention the entire time. Of course, that could've just been because it was a good book.

Nonetheless, over the next several weeks I slipped into a fairly decent—although not terribly satisfying—routine, and the extra money was a big help. I had no intention of being a substitute teacher for the rest of my life, but at the same time, I wasn't quite sure where I was going to go from there.

In the back of my mind I kept thinking that I should return to playing the piano every day, or start sending out business cards to local wedding venues, or just look up the date of The Madison Wedding and Event Professionals' next meeting and mark it in my calendar. But for whatever reasons, I never did any of those things.

One week really stood out. I spent Monday subbing for a PE class—and mostly standing around while the other PE teacher led the kids in shooting baskets or doing laps around the gym. On Tuesday I subbed for a French class and was pretty useless the few times a kid had a question about conjugating verbs. And on Wednesday I was asked to cover for the chorus teacher.

There was a plain but decent-looking upright piano in the front of the classroom. I thought about playing it for a few minutes before the kids showed up, but the idea made me feel tired and a little depressed. I knew it was going to be another unremarkable day of sitting in the back of the room, doing little more than basic crowd control. So I just focused on getting everything ready.

Mrs. Caldwell, the chorus teacher, left a DVD for me to show all the classes. It was a bunch of Bugs Bunny cartoon shorts set to classical music. I knew it would probably do a better job of keeping the kids' attention than the DVD about organelles, but it wasn't long enough to take up the entire period. I headed to the teachers' workroom and made a lot of copies of a musical terms word search that I'd found the night before.

Thankfully, I was right about the kids enjoying the cartoons and the morning went by pretty much as expected. I watched Elmer Fudd dressed up as a Viking over and over again, but I also managed to read a few pages of my book about a ditzy British woman with a shopping addiction. There were only two times during the entire morning that I had to be a correctional officer—which was better than most days. I had to ask one student to be quiet and another to stop kicking the chair in front of him.

I had the seventh grade girls' chorus for fifth period. When the DVD was finished I started passing out the word searches.

"Why do we have to do a word search?" asked a girl in the back row. "This is chorus. Why can't we sing?"

"Because we have a sub, so we have to do busywork!" someone called back.

"So what?" said the first girl. "We can sing without Mrs. Caldwell. Can't we sing Mrs. Sub Lady? Please?"

She had a point. It didn't matter if they did the worksheets or not, and if they sang, that would keep them happy for the rest of the period. "Well … I guess, if you want."

The girl wasted no time. She grabbed a black folder from under her chair, leaped out of her seat, and rushed to the front of the room. "All right everybody," she said, pulling a piece of music out of the folder and setting it on the podium, "we're all going to sing 'Hine Ma Tov.' " She clapped her hands a couple times. "Okay, ready? Go!" she said, waving her arms in the air twice.

With some amusement, I realized that she was like an older version of Angela.

There were about three different starting pitches and at least two different tempos. The class fumbled the first two lines of the song before fizzling out.

"What's our starting note, Jill?" someone called out.

"It's this ... hmmmm!" Jill hummed. "Ready? Go!" She flipped her fingers open at them like she was casting a magic spell.

The second try wasn't much better.

"This isn't working," announced a girl in the front row as she slumped down in her seat. "Let's just forget about it."

"No, come on." Jill was getting frustrated. "You guys just aren't paying attention."

"I don't think that note is right," someone else said. "It sounds too high."

A few girls started humming various notes. They all thought their note was the right one. It was almost painful to watch.

The girls were eager to sing and they had nice voices, but they were totally lost. Jill, for all her passion and leadership skills, was only twelve and she didn't know how to lead a chorus. They needed someone who could give them an intro, get them all in the right key, and start them off in a steady tempo.

"Here, let's try it again," Jill said. "Ready? Go!"

No one even bothered singing.

"Jill, you can't just yell *go* at us," someone said. "You have to give us a beat."

These girls need someone who can play the piano, I thought.

"At least I'm trying!" Jill snapped.

A wave of anger washed over me, taking me completely by surprise. I was angry at my college professors for trying to get rid of me rather than helping me improve and be successful. I was angry at Grace Reese for being so negative and nitpicky that she felt the need to publicly insult me instead of having the decency to speak to me privately—or even just being *gracious* enough to be happy that her daughter was happy. But most of all, I was angry at myself. I was angry that I'd given up and wasted over a decade not doing what I loved just because of one incident and one person's opinion. I was angry that I'd come so close to letting it happen again. And it was that very anger that fueled me to jump up from my seat and go to the front of the classroom.

"Here, Jill," I said, "let me have the music. I think I can help."

She handed me the music. Then she watched in wonder as I took it to the piano and sat down on the bench.

"All right," I called out, rolling a d minor chord all the way up the keyboard to get their attention. "I'm going to play the two measures before you come in, and I'll nod right at your entrance, okay?" Without waiting for a response, I dove in and began playing.

I didn't play the song perfectly, of course. I had to leave out a lot of notes, and I missed the b flat a couple times. But I was able to keep a steady beat and give them the basic chord structure and a strong bass line which is all they really needed.

By the time we'd finished, the looks on the girls' faced were different. There was happiness at having been saved from boring busywork, but there was also something more. They no longer just saw me as the generic Substitute Lady who sat in the back of the classroom and played babysitter.

"We didn't know you played the piano," one of them said.

"You should sub for us all the time," said another girl.

Most of the girls were nodding in agreement.

"Can we sing it again?" someone asked.

We had time to run through it once more. When the bell rang they gathered their things and headed for the doors, several of them still singing as they left.

"Bye Mrs. Hershey," said Jill with a wave and a little skip as she headed out the door.

"Yeah, bye Mrs. Hershey," a few others called over their shoulders. "Thank you."

"Bye, girls," I said. "You're very welcome."

During sixth and seventh periods I didn't even think about getting out the word searches. As the DVD was playing I borrowed someone's chorus folder and flipped through the music. Then, when it was finished, I announced, "Now, for the rest of the period we're going to sing through a couple of your pieces. Which one would you like to start with?"

At the end of the day I left a note for Mrs. Caldwell. I told her what a wonderful day everybody had and how much singing we did. I happily headed out of the classroom and down the hall, whistling as I took out my car keys and twirled them around my index finger.

I picked up Danny and Angela on the way home. Then, with a little help from Angela, I got right to work making spaghetti and meatballs for dinner. We even experimented a little by adding extra oregano and a tiny dash of Worcestershire sauce.

After dinner, I adjusted my settings with the school system. I didn't want to get any calls to sub the next day.

Instead, I spent the day writing letters and mailing business cards and flyers to eight local wedding venues. Then I looked up the date of the next Madison Wedding and Event Professionals luncheon and marked it on my calendar.

I also spent over two hours playing the piano. Because, of course, I had to practice a lot if I wanted to be a great wedding pianist.

Sixteen

Danny wandered into the kitchen one afternoon about a week later, just as the phone started ringing. "Can you make me some chocolate milk?"

"Sure," I said, opening the refrigerator door and snatching up the kitchen phone with my other hand. "Hello, Heather Hershey speaking."

"Hi Heather. My name is Kristen. I got your name from The Williams House, where I'm getting married this Saturday."

I swung the refrigerator door shut.

"Mom! You said you were going to make me some chocolate milk!"

"Hi Kristen," I said, holding my hand up to silence Danny. "How can I help you?"

"Mom!"

I pulled Angela's drawing of the ballerina-mermaid-unicorn tea party off the fridge and turned it around. I held the *Be Quiet Please*! side in front of Danny's face for a minute before putting it down on the counter.

"I know it's really short notice," said Kristen, "but our pianist fell and broke his wrist yesterday. Is there any way you could do it? The ceremony starts at five."

"Mom!" Danny said in a loud whisper.

I bopped him on the head with Angela's drawing.

"Yes," I said, "this Saturday is fine. I'd be happy to do it."

"You can?" she said. "Oh, thank you! I can't wait to tell Erica, my wedding planner. We've been going crazy trying to figure out what to do."

Erica? I thought. "I'm sorry, who did you say your wedding planner is?"

Danny went to the refrigerator. He pulled out the bottle of chocolate syrup and held it up. "Mom, is this the chocolate milk?"

I nodded and shooed him away as I grabbed a pencil and pad from a drawer and went over to the kitchen table.

"Erica Cantrell, from Magical Moments Event Planning" Kristen said. "Do you know her?"

"We've met a couple times. I'm not sure if she would remember me, though." In fact, I was hoping that she didn't remember me.

"She'll be so happy to hear that I found you."

I hoped she was right.

We chatted for a couple minutes and I wrote down all the details. Before we hung up, I said I'd touch base with her the day before the wedding.

Wow, not just a wedding, but a wedding where I would actually be working with Erica Cantrell, I thought. If I did a great job and impressed her it could lead to all kinds of referrals and connections. On the other hand, if I *didn't* impress her … I decided to try not to think about that.

Danny sat down next to me at the table. He was holding a blue plastic cup, making smacking sounds with his chocolate-smeared lips. "This is good chocolate milk. It's *really* chocolaty."

I peeked in his cup. It contained nothing but a huge blob of chocolate syrup. "Danny! That's not chocolate milk. That's what you mix in the milk to *make* chocolate milk!!"

He took another long sip and smacked his lips. "It's good. You should make it like this all the time." He took one last swig before wiping his face with his sleeve and bounding out the kitchen door.

I rinsed his cup in the sink and put it in the dishwasher. I was about to leave the kitchen, but I paused. I glanced at the refrigerator. Eh, what the heck, I thought.

I grabbed the chocolate syrup and squirted some into a mug. "Here's to second chances!" I raised my mug of syrup in the air before chugging it down.

Danny was right. It *was* good.

* * *

I'd done everything I could possibly think of to make sure the day would go well. I had a huge stack of music in my bag, and the book on the top of the stack had a piece of paper taped to the cover with a reminder to *TURN OFF CELL PHONE!* written in black marker. If the ceremony was delayed because the best man had to travel to the next state to fetch a forgotten ring, the piano music would play on. And I'd packed a little case with clips of different sizes.

The Williams House was an old two-story mansion with huge white pillars in one of the most expensive areas of Madison. The wrought iron gates at the entrance led to a long gravel driveway that eventually curved around a fountain and garden area with a patio in front of the brick and wood building.

I dropped my car off with the valet and walked past four white wooden rocking chairs on the patio. I opened the double beveled glass doors and stepped inside.

The front lobby had a fireplace and a couple couches. I started down the hallway, passing huge paintings hung on the brick walls as the hardwood floors creaked beneath me.

The ceremony ballroom had tall arched windows with gold valances, and there was a huge crystal chandelier in the center of the high ceiling. Rows of gold chairs with white bustles faced the front of the room which had a slightly raised hardwood platform. The baby grand piano was to the left of the platform.

I sat down at the piano and started setting everything up. I put the ceremony music in order, making sure each piece was neatly marked with a clip. Then I turned off my phone.

I was flipping to Canon in D when I heard heels clicking across the floor. Erica Cantrell was heading toward me. Wow, that woman sure walks fast, I thought. I scrambled to my feet, smiled, and tried to look as polished as possible.

"Are you Heather?" she asked with a barely perceptible smile as she looked down at her clipboard.

"Yes," I said. "You must be Erica."

She gave a slight nod without looking at me and gestured toward the entrance of the ballroom. "I'll be standing back there with the bridal party and will signal to you when it's time to begin the music for seating of mothers and grandmothers. My weddings always begin exactly on time, so be ready."

"Got it," I said, wishing I had something a little more intelligent to say.

"And then I'll continue to signal from there for the rest of the processional." She looked back at her clipboard. "There is no unity candle or sand ceremony, so your next cue is when the officiant announces the couple for the first time, which is when you begin the recessional music." She unclipped an envelope from her clipboard and handed it to me. "This is for you."

"Thank you, Erica," I said with a big smile. "I'm really happy to finally be …"

She'd already turned around and was whooshing back the way she'd come.

Huh, I thought. Well, at least I didn't make a *bad* impression. Maybe I can wow her during the ceremony.

Everything went like clockwork. I began playing the prelude music at 4:30. And, as promised, at exactly 5 Erica signaled to me from the hallway outside the ballroom that the mothers and grandmothers were about to be seated. She signaled me again when the bridesmaids were about to enter the room.

Thanks to my handy-dandy clips, I was able to flip from song to song without any trouble at all. I managed to play Canon in D while keeping an eye on the bridesmaids and Erica—so that I wouldn't miss her next cue.

When the final bridesmaid arrived at her spot and turned to face the guests I was all set to flip to the Bridal March. I looked in Erica's direction for official approval. No one was there. There were no more bridesmaids in strapless teal gowns carrying tangerine and cream bouquets with teal ribbons walking into the room, and the bride was nowhere in sight. And, even stranger, Erica had vanished.

I started to panic. Did I do something wrong? Was everyone waiting for me to play the Bridal March? No, wait. Erica would've cued me. Wouldn't she? Or did she mean that she would cue for the processional, but I was supposed to start the music for the bridal entrance myself? I tried to remember her exact words, but she'd come and gone so quickly and she hadn't said much.

Was it possible that another bridesmaid was entering and I just didn't see her? I flitted my eyes around the ballroom, but I didn't see anything to give me a clue. There was no movement at the entrance, no sign of more teal dresses to come, nothing.

What was going on? And more importantly, what should I do? Well, there wasn't much I *could* do except continue playing Canon in D and hope that something started making sense very soon.

So continue playing I did. At the same time, I craned my neck and leaned at different angles, trying to catch a glimpse of anything that might give me an indication of what was going on.

As I was leaning forward, I finally saw Erica. She was crouched on the floor next to another woman. They were both facing a little boy in a tiny suit. Of course—the ring bearer! I couldn't tell exactly what was happening, but a reasonable guess was that he was refusing to walk down the aisle and Erica and the other woman—his mother, maybe?—were trying, unsuccessfully, to convince him to do his job.

Okay, now that I knew what was happening, what should I do? I'd been playing Canon in D long enough for seven bridesmaids to enter. How much longer could everyone stand to listen to it? I couldn't switch to the Bridal March yet. Should I just start playing something else, or would that be awkward?

I shifted my weight, trying to get a better feel for what was going on. Surely something would happen soon, right? We couldn't just sit here waiting forever.

Poor kid, I thought. Maybe they should just give him a break and go on with the ceremony. It's too bad I can't help somehow, like try to musically coax him to … Wait a minute. What if … ? No. That's crazy. Or is it?

I took another look at the scene in the doorway. Things didn't appear to be improving. I decided to risk it. I played an arpeggio, changed keys, and dove into a graceful version of … the theme song to *Millie Mallard's Pond of Fun*.

I had no idea if most people would recognize it, or what they would think if they did. And for all I knew, this boy never watched the show, or maybe he even hated it. But I figured it couldn't be much worse than playing endless rounds of Canon in D.

As I was starting the second verse—which describes Millie Mallard's friends Sammy Snail and Tabitha Turtle—I saw the little boy strutting down the aisle. He was holding a satin pillow, smiling, and bobbing his head to the music.

I couldn't believe it! It really worked! A simple song had changed everything. An unhappy child was now happy. All the people in the packed room were probably both relieved and amused. And the ceremony could go on.

Millie Mallard and her friends had helped save the day. And I'd finally managed to do something impressive in front of Erica Cantrell. I was so excited I could barely keep from grinning through the entire ceremony.

After I played the recessional, the guests filed out and headed to the reception room. My work here was done. I gathered my things and practically bounced across the ballroom floor and down the hall.

Before I left, I wanted to say goodbye to Erica and tell her that I enjoyed working with her. She might even want to thank me for helping out and we'd have a quick laugh together as two wedding professionals bonding over an amusing incident, I thought.

I saw her in the hallway outside the reception. She was still holding her clipboard, watching the guests as they mingled and slowly made their way inside the room.

"Erica, I know you're busy, but I just wanted to say a quick goodbye before I leave," I said. "I'm so glad the song worked. I guess we lucked out on that one."

She looked annoyed. "What song?"

"During the processional," I said, surprised that she didn't know what I was talking about. "The ring bearer finally came down the aisle when I played the theme song from *Millie Mallard's Pond of Fun*. He must like that show as much as my kids did when they were younger."

"Oh, *that*," Erica said. She leaned toward me and lowered her voice. "I keep telling couples not to involve kids in the ceremony, but they never listen. They think it'll be sooo cute." She rolled her eyes. "So what happens? Not only does the precious child hold up the entire ceremony, but now we all have to listen to kiddie songs. I work hard to get these weddings just right." She grimaced and looked into the reception room as she bobbed her head back and forth and pointed her index finger at people in the distance, counting. "I don't appreciate having my work ruined by some little kid."

I was speechless. Not that it mattered, because it didn't look like Erica was interested in anything I had to say.

As I watched Erica jot something down on her precious clipboard, I realized she was indeed the president of Madison Wedding and Event Professionals, and the owner of Magical Moments Event Planning, but she was not a nice person. She cared less about the actual people whose weddings she was planning than she did about making herself look good. She cared less about forming relationships with her colleagues and more about charming people who would help serve her interests.

Erica Cantrell was not someone I would want planning my wedding. In fact, she was not someone I particularly wanted to work with again. And I certainly didn't need her help or approval.

"Well," I said, although I doubted she was listening, "I'm just glad that I could be part of their special day." And with that, I turned around and proudly walked down the hallway toward the front of the building.

The ring bearer was sitting on a couch in the lobby with a couple of boys a little older than him. They were laughing, poking each other, and just generally acting silly. I gave them a big smile before I pushed open the double doors and handed my parking ticket to the valet so I could head home to my family.

Seventeen

In early May Stephanie and I were sitting on her back patio at table with an umbrella. She was sorting through a big bin of art supplies in her lap, and I had my usual diet soda in hand. The kids were at a nearby picnic table on the grass, wrapping rubber bands around trays.

"So something really cool happened yesterday," I said to Stephanie. "I got an email from the chorus teacher at Streams High School. She said she got my name from someone named Meg Caldwell."

"Who's Meg Caldwell?" Stephanie was pulling bottles of squeeze paint out of her bin one by one and setting them on the table.

"That's what I couldn't figure out at first. But when I read it the second time I realized it was *Mrs.* Caldwell, the chorus teacher I subbed for that day. Remember?"

"Sure," Stephanie said. "Hey kids, go ahead and put on your aprons and goggles, and then come get your paints." She turned back to me. "So did she want you to sub for her chorus class too?"

"No, even better," I said as all four kids came over to the patio and grabbed bottles of different colored squeeze paint. "She said she needed an accompanist for her spring chorus concert in two weeks and wanted to see if I could do it. I guess Mrs. Caldwell was impressed with whatever the kids told her about me."

"Hey, that's great." Stephanie tied her hair back into a ponytail and picked up a floral apron. "Are you joining us?" she asked as she slid a pair of plastic goggles onto her head and stood up.

"I think I might just be a spectator for this one."

"Okay. Just let us know if you change your mind." She put her apron on, grabbed a pile of white paper, and walked over to the kids' table. "Did you guys get plenty of paint all over your rubber bands?"

"Yup," Angela said.

"And on our hands," said Danny as he and Trevor held them up as proof.

"Perfect. Now just hang on a minute while I slide the papers onto your trays," said Stephanie. "Okay, ready?"

"Ready!" all four kids called out.

"And … go!" Stephanie yelled.

They started snapping the rubber bands and paint of all colors went flying everywhere. All five of them were shrieking and laughing.

"Um … this paint is washable, right?" I asked as a big orange blob flew through the air and landed on the edge of the patio.

"Sure!" Stephanie yelled as she pulled back one of Katie's rubber bands as far as it would go and let it pop.

"Come join us Mommy!" called Angela. She already had green paint smeared in her hair.

"Thanks, but I'll just watch," I called back. "I'm not sure that this is exactly my thing. It looks like fun, though."

"It's awesome!" Danny yelled as he angled his tray and snapped a rubber band right at Trevor.

"Can I have another piece of paper?" Katie asked.

"Yup, there's plenty," said Stephanie. "Here, let me just slide this one out and put it down over here. Okay, you're all set."

"Come on Mommy!" Angela called again. "You should at least try it."

I watched her laugh as she plucked a couple of rubber bands and let them snap. Danny was running across the grass trying to dodge some paint that was flying right at him.

I quickly slid on an apron and goggles and went running through the grass to join them.

*   *   *

As the start of the next school year approached I was thinking about everything that had changed over the past year. I was also reminded of one special person.

I decided to see if I could find her. I knew now that teaching was really hard, and often thankless. She deserved to know what a difference she'd made in my life.

August 28

Dear Mrs. Casey,

Do you remember me? My name is Heather Collins and you were my piano teacher for many years while I was growing up.

I was able to find you through the magic of the Internet, but wanted to take the time to write you a handwritten note instead of just emailing you.

I currently live in Madison with my husband Steve and our two kids. Angela is about to start fourth grade and Danny will be in second grade.

These past twelve months have been pretty exciting for me and my family. Not only have I started playing the piano again for the first time in years, but I'm actually working as a musician now. So far I've played for five weddings and am already booked to play for three more this fall and winter. It was pretty challenging at first, but I'm getting the hang of it the more I do it.

What's also exciting is that this school year I will be working as a part-time choral accompanist for two of the high schools in our district. This is perfect because I can work during the hours that my kids are in school. I'm also looking forward to getting to know the high school kids that I'll be working with.

I wanted to thank you for all the years you taught and encouraged me. When I was a kid I didn't think much of it, but now I'm starting to realize what an important role you had in my life and how much that means to me, even all these years later.

I imagine that being a teacher is a lot like being a mother. You do the best you can, sometimes you feel like you're doing a terrible job, and you often wonder if the work you do makes any difference at all.

I want to assure you that yes, it does.

Heather Collins Hershey

*   *   *

Steve and I were sitting at a picnic table one afternoon.

"Come on, kids," I called to the playground. "We're gonna eat now."

Danny leaped off his swing in mid-air. Angela dragged her heels on the ground for a few seconds before hopping off hers.

"This was a good idea, to come to the park today," Steve said as we watched the kids running toward us. "It's going to start getting too cold for the park soon."

And the kids will be too old for playing at the playground soon, or relatively soon, at least, I thought. In a few years they'll be spending their Saturdays going out with their friends, or working at their part-time jobs, or doing their homework—not going on a picnic with their parents and swinging on the swings together. It was hard to believe, but I knew it was true.

Danny climbed up on the bench next to Steve. "What's for lunch?" he asked as he slipped into the seat.

"Nothing fancy," I said, opening the picnic basket and arranging the food and bottles of water on the table. "Just turkey sandwiches and grapes."

Danny grabbed a few grapes and stuffed them in his mouth.

"Mommy! Daddy!" Angela waved her arms to get our attention. "Did you know I learned how to do a cartwheel this week? Abby showed me how during recess. Look!" She pointed her toe, scrunched up her face in concentration, and then did her best cartwheel.

Her feet barely got off the ground. It looked more like a squat with a bounce.

Steve and I exchanged amused looks.

"Here, let me do it again!" She turned another something-that-wasn't-quite-a-cartwheel, then stood up with her arms raised above her head. "Ta-da!"

"Very nice," I said.

She sat down and took her sandwich out of the bag, obviously very pleased with herself. "I think I'm going to be a gymnast when I grow up."

"And I'm gonna be a fireman," Danny said with his mouth full.

I looked at my son and daughter happily munching away. It was as if I was looking at them for the first time. They were each so different—and so special—in their own ways. I didn't know if they'd ever become a gymnast or a fireman. But I hoped that, whatever they chose to pursue, they would always retain the joy that I saw in their faces in that moment.

I reached across the table and took Steve's hand in mine. I smiled at him before I turned back to the kids. "We think that's great," I said. "And we'll always be here cheering for both of you."

Acknowledgements

A special thanks to the following people:

My husband Robert for encouraging and supporting me while I wrote this book and getting me back on track whenever I freaked out about technical issues.

Our children Rachael, Rebecca, and Benjamin for helping me come up with some of the characters' names, and, with the help of their friend Maggie Sides, coming up with the title *Millie Mallard's Pond of Fun.*

My wonderful editor Tara Keogh at The OCD Editor.

My very patient cover designer Ana Grigoriu. In addition, my daughter Rebecca for coming up with the original book cover concept, Robert Blaske pointing out details I never would have noticed myself, and Linda Tenny, who suggested we add a coffee mug and stuffed animal to the piano.

Rachel Reminh, Mary Beth Marion, Nicole Bezerra, Shelley Lorah, Rebecca Brewster Steveson, Ali Puch, and Steve Smith, who were all willing to look at some or all of this book in its early stages.

And my "British email mentor" Caro Clarke, who I contacted after enjoying her articles on writing advice. Without her, this book probably wouldn't exist.

Visit the Real Wedding Musician Mom of Atlanta

Although this book is a work of fiction, it was obviously inspired by my years of playing the piano for weddings and other special events.

If you'd like to read true tales of my piano adventures, see and hear me "in action," or sign up for my mailing list to get early info about my next books, please visit **www.PianoJenny.com**.

Made in the USA
Middletown, DE
18 September 2016